RANDOM THOUGHTS FROM A RANDOM GUY

Cory S. Duran

ISBN: 1539353192
ISBN 13:9781539353195

This book is dedicated to everyone I have ever called friend. Please know the love in my heart for you is always there, even during the bad and misunderstood times. Your friendships have molded me into the man I am today, and I sincerely thank you.

A few years back, a close friend of mine called and said, "You should write a book." I said, "Why would you say that?" She replied, "Well, you seem to feel the pulse of the people. It's like you know what people are thinking and how to get people to see the things they don't want to see." Well, my dear, you got what you wished for: a book by the most random of people, a book of complete randomness.

I would like you to think of this as an adventure into the mind of a thinker, the mind of a lover, the mind of the guy next door, but mostly the mind of a friend. First, let me tell you, I'm not a scholar or someone who will put a lot of thought into what I write. However, what you will get is the raw truth from my point of view. Once again: random thoughts from a random guy. So before we dive into the mind of said random guy, let me tell you a little bit about myself.

Quite frankly, in my mind, I'm a pretty big deal—until I walk out in the real world and realize no one even pays attention to me. And if I'm even more honest about myself, I'm rather boring, but I have a mind like no other. I dream in 4K HD with Dolby Digital THX surround sound, and things in life just seem obvious and clear to me. I love from the deepest depths of my soul and have an unrelenting desire to always be the best. I'm from a humble background, not rich and not poor. I'm the kid who got the new bike but wore Polo Club shirts and never owned a pair of Jordans. I'm not the smartest, but I'm definitely not dumb or uneducated in most matters of life, love, and random facts. Mostly I am a man of the people and a friend of loyalty and the truth. I don't see the world in only black and white; I believe everything comes down to right and wrong. I will write only about my own life and the experiences I have seen through my eyes. I have traveled the world, seen many things, and met many people. My opinions are shaped by the teachings and lessons of the many people I have met on this rock. See, I'm a firm believer that you can learn something from every man or woman you meet. It doesn't matter who they are or what path they have walked—everyone has something they can give to this crazy world of ours.

So, randomly, I woke up and decided to write to the world and spread a message of love, happiness, and hope. Let me be that random guy who shares his stories and experiences for the benefit of all humanity. Well, maybe not all of humanity, but the twenty or so people who will be brave enough to read my words. Yeah, I know what you are thinking: corny, crazy, and stupid. OK, maybe just a little, but that's the cool part about this. We are about to embark on a journey of crazy stories and thoughts on love, life, and common sense. I ask only that you keep an open mind and prepare yourself for smiles, random thoughts, conversation, and the longest run-on sentence in the history of writing. So let's jump into these random thoughts.

SEX, LIES, AND INSTAGRAM

Let's start with the never-ending story of boy meets girl. Dating today is such a joke—and, in truth, the biggest con game in the world. We have all seen the old movies where a guy sees a girl across the room. They stare at each other and spark a conversation about family, life, love, and all those subjects. They leave and continue the conversation walking in the park, with laughter and joy filling the air. Fast-forward to a few weeks later, and they are happily married and preparing for a long life together. Where does this shit happen in the real world? Today's dating scene has become a big joke because everyone is faking their way through it. The problem is that there are too many options available for everyone. Let me try to explain, but first let's look toward the past.

Long ago, things were simple, and relationships were arranged by the family. Most of the time it was strategic to connect one family to another for a reason that had nothing to do with love. You were forced to work with what was presented to you. Now I'm not saying we should go back to those days, but one effect of arranged marriages was that people were forced to work harder to make a relationship work because of the newly created family ties. Nowadays people date for months and even years before they even meet the family. Moving up to more modern times, people would date people from the same neighborhood or school. It was like a musical chairs version of dating—or my guilty pleasure, *Bachelor in Paradise*—with everyone fighting for the same people and the losers taking the leftovers.

Today's online world offers plenty of options for dating and meeting people: OkCupid, POF (Plenty of Fish), eHarmony, Match, Coffee Meets Bagel, and the infamous Tinder. Even with all these choices, people still find themselves saying dumb shit like, "It's so hard to meet good people!" It is hard because we know if things are not perfect with our first pick, we can try again. This form of dating makes us weak and impatient to look beyond the superficial. We should not be so quick to quit when one thing doesn't go right in a new relationship or introduction. I have been guilty of this myself, so I can understand and know how easy it is to fall for the trap. Lately I have found myself in digital relationships with people I have never met in the physical form. I don't know their true complexion because of the filters they use to edit their pics. I do not know the sounds of their laughter when they truly laugh out loud.

For example, I happened to be out at this event and recognized someone I follow on Instagram. I said to myself, "Wow, it's @somerandomchick69, and she is even more gorgeous in person." I've followed her page for a year or so and thought she was a beautiful woman, the kind who, in my head, was nothing short of perfection. She had this exotic look and seemed to be fun and charismatic with a hint of mystery. I wanted to walk up and just start talking as if we were old friends. Then I realized, after I felt myself staring too long, that I don't know this girl and she doesn't know me. Sure, maybe she liked my pic once or twice and even said thank you to a comment, but she is as much a stranger to me as Halle Berry or

Scarlett Johansson, just a pretty and familiar face. In today's world it's easy to get lost in the idea that because people follow you on social media or like your picture, you actually have a chance to know them personally. However, it's mostly the opposite, in that we may never know them or even have a chance. Unfortunately, this daily interaction with social media has ruined dating in modern times.

In my younger days, my dream girl was the *Playboy* bunny, the *Maxim* or *FHM* cover girl, or even the *JET* Beauty of the Week, all of whom I lusted and yearned for in my dreams. Now all I have to do is log into Facebook, Snapchat, or Instagram to see beautiful centerfold-type women locally and globally. The only difference is that the social-media vixen is real, and with a little mild stalking, I can be where she is for that 1 percent chance she will look into my eyes, and we can begin our fairy-tale story of meeting and falling in love.

A story comes to mind of my experience with social-media dating, but I want to preface it by saying that all relationships started in this manner are not doomed to failure—only the ones based on the lie that your digital self is the same as your real-life self. I say this because most people will never post the negative parts of their lives and personality. So when I see a woman post a picture of herself eating pizza, drinking beer on the sofa in pj's, a big pimple on her nose, no makeup, and smiling without duck lips, only then will I propose marriage. Until then I have to believe that anyone I see online is only showing me half of who he or she really is—with self-narrated subtitles.

Now back to my story. So there was this one time at band camp... OK, I'm joking to see if you are paying attention to this deep line of thought. Thinking about your failures at dating is sometimes a hard task to take on, but you have to laugh at the experiences and learn from them. Anyway, on to the story. Mark Zuckerberg and his Facebook generals added a feature called People You May Know, probably based on friends of your friends. One day, up pops a beautiful face, but I soon learned how a single click can cause pain and heartbreak. After sending her a friend request and her accepting my digital friendship, I became hypnotized by her beauty. There was something in her smile that attracted me to her, and the man in me wanted to know more than her social-media profile. I wanted to know her likes and dislikes, her experiences, and the things that made her happy. In short, without ever meeting her or even seeing her in person, I was in love. Love at first sight, I'm not so sure, but love at first click or view is a better way of putting it.

After a few weeks of checking out her pics and liking her posts and pictures, I decided to send her message and request a formal meet and greet, live and in person. This wasn't something I had done before, because I've never been good at asking women out, in person or digitally. I sat on my sofa and typed out this short and straight-to-the-point message. *I think you are beautiful and want to meet you. Let's do lunch sometime and formally meet.* Wasn't that hard to send, and I assumed that based on her friendly digital projection in her pics and posts, she would reply promptly, and we would meet. After a day or two went by with no reply, I checked to see if she had read my message. She had and didn't reply, so at this point, I was heartbroken and feeling rejected. How could she not reply? I changed my cover photo so she would see the best pic of me. I posted love poems and quotes so she knew I was a nice guy and not some crazy lunatic.

Weeks turned to months, months turned into a year, and still no reply. During that time, I had been out on several dates but nothing serious. However, it was very strange that no matter who I dated, I found myself thinking of this beautiful yet mysterious woman I had never met. It had been a while since I viewed her page and even longer since she had liked any of my pics or posts. Ladies, please know that we men do notice things like who is liking our pics. In our minds, if you like our pics, you must like us and want to have our babies. Maybe not that serious, but we do notice who is paying attention to our profiles. Not too many men will admit it, but men can be just as self-centered and vain as women.

I decided to check out her page and see if there was anything new with her. Boom, there it was, the answer to all my fears: she was in a relationship. So one minute I'm viewing her as if she were the most perfect creature on the planet and next thinking, WTF! Briefly heartbroken and rejected and beginning to doubt myself, but I paused and said, "Oh well, wasn't meant to be." During that time, I had made a career change and got out of a really complicated relationship, so for a short moment, I thought I had found the woman of my dreams without ever hearing her say my name. As I stated earlier, it is really hard to write down your failures in relationships, mostly because when you think back, you feel like a complete dumbass. When it comes to matters of the heart, the heart wants what it wants, and the brain will never convince the heart otherwise.

After discovering this news about her relationship, I put her out of my mind. I didn't unfriend her, but I did unfollow her because I didn't want to see pictures of her and her boyfriend in my timeline. It was a small and gentle stab that I was not good enough. My actions were petty and immature, but who says I have to be mature when my crush doesn't give me a chance or even reply?

Let's fast-forward a few months to a day where I had long conversation with my friend and coworker about dating, about how I'm not going to date anymore, and how the next girl I date will have to come after me. "I'm Rick James, Bitch!" (my Facebook message ringtone) started playing, and I looked down at my phone slightly confused—who was messaging me at that time of day? I wasn't dating anyone, and at that time, I only expected messages from family members or spammers. To my amazement and surprise, it was my mystery digital now-has-a-boyfriend girl. She replied to my message and apologized for not replying sooner. Could this really be happening? My dream girl was reaching out with the same intentions I had a year earlier? I was happy and surprised, but I hesitated because experiences have burned me, and I didn't want that feeling again.

After reading and overanalyzing her message, I checked her relationship status. Just as big and bold as when I looked the first time: IN A RELATIONSHIP. WTF! I was confused and yet tempted by the idea that the girl I have crushed over was interested in knowing more about me. So I decided I would be smart and just go with the flow. That sounded so much better in my head than what would happen in the following weeks. After we traded several messages, she gave me her number without me even asking for it. That had to be a good sign, right? Our phone conversations were long and frequent, and we would discuss everything under the moon but the most obvious topic was this: Are you still in a relationship? I'll be honest—I didn't want ask, as I knew the truth would be painful, and I wanted things to work with this woman. She was smart, fun, easy to talk with, and very beautiful. Finally, after numerous messages and conversations, I decided to ask her out on a formal meet and greet. She agreed, and to say I was the happiest man in the world at that time would have been a big understatement.

We agreed on a place and time, but there was something I very much needed to do before we met. I had to ask the question I didn't want to hear the answer to. In our next conversation, I didn't waste time; I just put it out there. "So what's going on with your situation?" That was pretty much the laziest way to ask a direct question, but I didn't want to ruin all the good vibes we had established while talking. She gave me what I saw at the time as a good, respectable answer: she and her boyfriend had broken up because he had cheated on her not once but twice. She didn't want to change her status because she didn't want her friends, family, and coworkers to be all in her business. She wanted to move on on her own terms and deal with the drama of the breakup without her digital family (she knew people would see the change in her relationship status and would be all up in the Kool-Aid). How could I not respect her answer and understand where she was coming from? But how could I not see that was such a scapegoat answer and that she was fighting her own internal battles? Remember, her digital projection was happy, smiling, and joyful, but after talking with her and finally meeting her, it wasn't the same story.

In our first meeting, we sat and talked over dinner, and I found her to be shy, reserved, and wounded. Wounded not just from her last relationship but from her relationship with every man of any importance in her life. Past relationships, her family, her father, her stepfather, it didn't matter—men had given her hell, and she was in search of something better. I looked into her eyes that night and felt her pain. I wanted to put my arms around her and say, "You don't have to worry anymore. Look at my cape flapping in the wind. I'm here to save you and make everything better." I instead grabbed her hand, and she held mine, and we briefly connected in the physical and spiritual energy of hope and optimism. She told me the story of how her last boyfriend lied to her and how she felt cheated by his lies. Her eyes were glassy with tears from the pain of remembering the hurt he caused. Something about those tears gave me pause, and I pulled my hand back to think about this moment. Tears over a lie, tears over a cheat, and tears from the pain he had caused while sitting here with a guy who you know likes you. There was something strange about that moment as I sat there and thought that situation out more.

The experienced dater in me came to a fast conclusion: she is still in love with this guy. As I said before, the heart wants what the heart wants. Arrogantly, I chose to ignore my gut and prove to her I could be the man she longed for in her dreams. I fooled myself into believing I could fix this moment for her and bring her happiness and joy on a level she had never experienced. How foolish can a man be when it comes to a woman?

I said to myself that I wouldn't bring up the ex, but I would from time to time check on the relationship status to see how things were going. It would be my clue to see how things were going with us, because if we were going to be an item, then the status would have to change. That is fair and rational thinking; at least I wanted to believe that.

Our dates became numerous and longer as each week went by. We truly enjoyed each other's company, and the laughter was constant. We would stay on the phone until one or two in morning even during the week. How could I not fall for her and she for me? I sent flowers to her job because I wanted her to know how special she was to me. She even posted them online for her friends to see. That made me so happy because it was a good sign that she was proud of my gesture of love. After that I decided to step my game up, as I knew her birthday was near, and I wanted her to know I really cared about her. I wanted her to know without question that I wanted to be her man. I wanted to be the guy who never caused her pain; I wanted to be her last first kiss and the key to a happy future with doubt and heartache.

For her birthday, I planned a wonderful dinner date and got a gift of appreciation to show my intentions were sincere and genuine. I happened to be out of town that day, but I knew I would be back to celebrate with her that evening. She was off that day and said she was going to rest up and get ready for dinner.

After returning home from my trip, I decided to rest up and relax before our date, as I wanted the night to be perfect. I arranged with the restaurant for a good table with a view. I had been around her long enough to notice her fashion sense, so I picked out a lovely watch I knew she would love. I also bought the prettiest long-stemmed red roses I could find because I wanted the night to be special. I wanted her to walk away from this date knowing without a doubt she had found the man of her dreams. That's where this story takes a detour and ends up in a place of confusion and hurt. Lying in bed before our date, I decided to post a happy-birthday note on her Facebook timeline. Nothing overpowering, just a small note to say happy birthday. What a surprise did I have coming.

The first post I saw before I started to write is from her supposedly ex-boyfriend saying how much he loved her and how he couldn't wait to see her later. Wait, did I miss something? I thought they had broken up. I thought he cheated on her and broke her heart. I thought we were having dinner. I thought things were moving in the right direction for us. As it turns out, I was the blind one; I was the one confused by my relationships with women. I was the one who openly gave my heart to someone still in love with a confessed liar and cheat. How could I overcome that kind of emotion and affection with a stupid dinner and a worthless gift?

I was hurt and confused that she left out this vital information about her situation with him. I know I was clear in telling her about my past and thought she was clear in telling me hers. So why would she subject me to the same emotions that haunted her from his actions? I was pissed that I had let this happen to me, but I agreed to dinner after speaking with her. I was bitter and pretty pissed off, but I had my heart set on steak, and dammit, I was going to eat steak!

Dinner was very emotional to say the least, and her tears were making the entire restaurant uncomfortable. I just wanted to eat my medium-rare steak and enjoy the jazz playing in the background. Yes, I wanted I cry and wanted to be mad at her. I wanted to get up and walk out, leaving her there to know the pain and hurt she had caused. Guess the hopeless romantic in me wouldn't allow it and just sat there wishing I could take her tears away. I sat there admiring her beauty and sensing through the pain, tears, and lies she really did care for me. Hard to believe, after that day turned out, that I still had feelings for this woman. I found myself wanting to try harder to convince her that I was the man she needed, and her ex-boyfriend was all wrong and a complete fraud. Not sure what spell she put on me, but it was some strong magic to have me wanting to be there for her. She had spent the last few months living a lie, using me, and taking my ability to choose this situation away. Had I known her true situation, I could have chosen to continue or not. Taking my choice away, she essentially stole my heart without me having a say in the matter. She left me standing there with my heart in my hand yearning for answers. However, the answer was there the whole time, and I was the fool to believe anything else.

Days and weeks have gone by, and yes, she is still in my life. In truth, she will always be because I do still love her and want nothing but the best for her. Things are different between us now because she puts me inside of a box and doesn't share all of her emotions with me. However, when we get together and she sits across from me, for a second I see love and her regret over not choosing me. It's that little shimmer of hope that allows me to know that she is worth all the heartache. Guess I will always be her what-if guy, and sometimes that's good enough.

In this situation, I learned so much about dating in the digital world. Although we bonded and connected in the physical world, it was her digital self that kept me from thinking logically. The smiles in her pictures felt like they were for me. The emojis of kisses and blushed faces felt so sincere, but it all goes back to the old saying, "Actions speak louder than words." Her words said she cared about me and even loved me. But her actions said she loved him more, and nothing I could do would change that.

We all have to remember that "actions" in that old saying is plural. One or two actions of love in your favor cannot be good enough when everything isn't adding up. We must pay attention to the signs on the road trip to love—Stop, Yield, Railroad Crossing, Liars, and Cheats Ahead—and open our eyes to the rules of the dating road.

Bucket List

I have this list of things in my head that I want to do and achieve: own an NBA team, walk on the moon, and travel at warp speed. Yes, all crazy and will never happen beyond my own head and dreams. However, those wild dreams motivate me daily. My more reasonable bucket list items are have a beach house, own big boat to fish daily, fall in love, and backpack the Pacific Trail. Also, I think about having the ability to travel anywhere in the world at any time without thoughts of cost. These are the things that I wake up almost every day and think about and wish for myself. There have been many times when I have talked to people and their thoughts only go a few hours or days ahead. Ask them about their life plans and they look at you like you are crazy—they are only thinking about their life for the moment and not the long haul. People think about silly things like "I'm going to work hard all week just to have a few beers at bar over the weekend." Of course, we should always think about our current issues and where we are in life currently, but we have to have dreams. Those wild and crazy dreams give us purpose and something to work toward. I may never get a chance to fly to and explore another galaxy, but I will work as hard as if I will. I don't want my life to be a Rihanna song, work, work, work, work. I want my life to have moments that can become memories and dreams. Even if some of the things on my list are farfetched, I still find myself hoping and wishing for some of them. I beg everyone to make a list of the things you would love to do. Make it crazy and wild or make it something reasonable, but just make a list of the things you would love to do. Just keep dreaming big and work your ass off to check a couple of things off of your list. I'm sure that your dreams will thank you for it!

Bad Cupid

I ask myself if Cupid is a hero or a villain. Seriously, let's think about this. A little man with a bow and arrow and very bad aim.

He always seems to hit me right in my ass with a jolt of crazy at the wrong moment. I see love all around me, people getting married, loving each other, sexing each other, but then I wonder if this was Cupid or some sick trick to teach me a lesson. Step away for a second and think about all the relationships you have been in, and now think about all the relationships you wish you could trade in for an iTunes gift card. We all have had moments where we look back and wonder, "What the hell was I thinking about?" Yes, things were fine at the moment we met, but "fine" changed to "crazy," and "crazy" changed to "call the police" really quick. Yet still we ignored our inner voice and kept going with the crazy no matter how wrong we thought it was. I'm going to dive deeper into the inner voice later, but for now know that our inner voice usually is right more times than not.

I would like to tell a story, a story about life and love. How love can give you life, and how life can destroy love. We all have dreamed of the soul mate or of the perfect partner. In most cases, that person is shaped by many factors starting with our perceived image of beauty from media outlets, to our family members who we relate love to. See, love has a place in everyone's life, but mostly its place will be determined only by a person letting go of fear and opening the heart, mind, and soul to love's full potential. I smile thinking about the potential of love, as it has the ability to change so much in this world. However, we as a people ignore its potential in favor of more juvenile emotions of the heart: fear, hate, jealousy are triplets of destruction in any life and love decisions.

My story begins by falling in love with life but not in love with the person who loved me. How easy it is to get caught up in ourselves and ignore the people who truly have our back and love us. I think back to a time where I became attracted to the idea of a person because of her beautiful exterior and ignored everything else. Everyone thought this woman was the most beautiful thing in the world. However, every time I was around her she made my skin crawl. The only smile she knew was the one that got her money, dinner, or attention. She always viewed life as if the world owed her something for not doing anything. The only thing she was good at was being pretty, and even that was in question because of her attitude. I don't want to demonize a person, but we all know that type never has anything good to say. This situation with this woman went from zero to one hundred in the worst way, and memories of will forever haunt me. Not because she left some scar on my spirit, but because I didn't stay true to my values.

During this time, the voice in my head said, "Something is very wrong here, and you need to remove yourself." Each time I would make an excuse and try to see the good in her with the hope that she would change, but in hindsight I know more than anything that people never change. They might learn new actions or emotions to hide their true selves, but people will always be who they are inside. If you are a mean and hateful person down to your core, you will more than likely always be that way. Her negative vibes caused me to make business mistakes and cost me friendships, all because I felt I could help her become a more loving and gentle person. I felt that I could save her and take away her pessimism about life and people. I'm not sure if I ever loved her, but I'm sure that I cared enough to be there for her and her family. Even when she allowed things and people to hurt me, I stayed loyal to her. Loyal to her but deaf and blind to my gut that kept screaming for me to cut my losses and walk away.

I share this story because I'm sure we all have blindly loved or lusted after another person, but it has to be more than lust and love. There will always be things and people in life that just don't add up to success. Your spirit will warn you, your gut will tell you—hell, even your eyes won't be fooled—so it's important to just stop and listen. There will be times to take a risk on love and just try to help someone. However, you can never compromise yourself or lose yourself trying to help or save someone. Who will save you when you are drowning in your own stupidity? So next time you see Cupid flying around and taking aim, don't forget to duck and get out of the way. Real love will find you, and you don't need a flying fat guy to help you.

Love

Have you ever woken up with a bad feeling in your stomach? Slight temperature and the urge to go to the bathroom? As the day progresses, things seem to go downhill, and your symptoms change for the worse. Your breathing changes, your heart rate increases, and your appetite decreases. You keep going as if everything is fine, but deep down you get the feeling that you are on the verge of coming down with something. Not knowing what it is, you opt for rest and try to cut the feeling with a glass of whiskey. What could this feeling of inconvenience be—a cold, something trivial like gas? More than likely it is an emotion that we all fear and wish to deny: love.

Love is the root of all evil, not money. Love of country, love of money, love of food, love of woman or man, or the best one, love of ass. Love is an emotion that can take the strongest person and make them weak. We all have fought hard to ignore it, and there are times when we try to embrace it. However, no matter our courage, love will always win in the battle for our hearts. I am one of those people who are very comfortable with the idea of love but not the application of it. I think we all want to find something or someone one to love. We want to have that love given back to us in return. However, in applying love to others, we open ourselves to rejection, pain, and heartbreak. Tell people you love them when they are not ready to hear it, and watch them run for the hills. Act as if you don't care, and see them fight hard for your trust and love. It's the emotion of love that makes all things great but equally tears things apart. Love of money gives us motivation to push our abilities to achieve things professionally. That same love of money can corrupt our spirits and make us lie and cheat our way to achievement. Love of a person can cause you to be blind to flaws, making a fool out you. Isn't love supposed to be gentle and kind, not mean and destructive? Why does such a beautiful thing cause so much headache and heartbreak?

The answer is simple if you understand what love is and what it is not. Love is a virus that will infect all parts of your body and spirit. However, true love's infection will not cause you pain or misery, only joy and pleasure. If you ever have to ask yourself if it is love, or if you can walk away from it without hesitation, it more than likely wasn't love. If you always find yourself feeling like you need more and deserve better, then it isn't love. Love will provide everything you need, and you will always feel its presence. In your profession, in your friendships, in family, in relationships, love is always the answer but never the cure. The cure comes from understanding what love is and what it isn't. The passion that comes from love gives anyone the proof that love is there, and you will never have to doubt its presence. Just don't ever put yourself in a situation where you are forcing love to happen. By forcing, I mean you are making compromises in order to achieve what you feel is love. We see people all the time blindly falling in love and ignoring someone's flaws, telling themselves that they can live with this flaw, or they will change to make the situation better.

I can always tell real love from fake love in others. The fake lovers will broadcast their affection so others will believe that they are in love. You know, showing pictures on social media of selfie kisses or weekend getaways to show everyone they are in love. However, that always looks staged and so fake you almost have to laugh at the

PDA (public display of affection). Think about the cute old couple walking through the mall or eating dinner at a restaurant. No hand holding, no kisses for others to see. Think about the couple that always together and enjoying each other without tripping over each other. Their love seems to have the admiration and slight envy of their peers. In both examples, that is what real love looks like and feels like. You don't have to show it or prove it to others because everyone already knows. Body language is everything, and if you have to force others to see it, you might be forcing something that isn't real.

Maybe one day it might become love for you, but trust and believe you have not found it yet. The love jones we all seek in some variation comes when we are not looking for it but when our heart and mind are ready for it. Be brave and take a chance on love because love, in its purest form, will always win. So next time someone says they love you, it's OK to question it, but the answers are there for you to see. Just open your eyes and see the truth right in front of you.

What Would You Do?

What would you do if you went to a store and the employees followed you as you shopped? What would you do if your son or daughter was involved in a police-related shooting? What would you do if your homeland was taken over by outsiders from another land? What would you do if you lived in fear because of your sexual identity or whom you loved? What would do if you were paid to protect and serve but people disrespected you at every opportunity? What would you do if someone judged you based on someone else's actions? What would you do if you lost everything that was important to you, and you had no more options? What would you do if you lost your best friend to a Tinder match? What would do if you lost your job to someone with no experience and who was the son of your manager? What would you do if people only saw your boobs and not your mind? What would you do if people stared at you because you were different and you embraced your weirdness? What would you do if you truly had to walk a mile in someone else's shoes? What would you do?

It is so easy in today's world for people to have an opinion on someone's actions, reactions, or emotions, but how can you truly know what you would do? While writings these words, I have seen protests concerning police actions in my area. I watch and see so many opinions in regards to people taking sides and passing judgment. Personally, I think many matters are never purely right or wrong—there is always more to a story than what you see with your own eyes. Many things are never as simple as someone is wrong or someone is right. There is always more to a story, and to truly understand, you must always look at the big picture. The big picture can be a very hard experience if you take a strong stance on a subject based on emotions and not facts. How can we place judgment on another person and their beliefs if we haven't taken a step back and looked at all the information?

I will be bold and say I don't understand transgender identification at all. However, I openly accept someone's right to identify with and even change to another gender. I am not God, and I have no business telling people how to live their lives. Maybe they are right, and maybe they will be judged by a higher power, but I have no business telling any man or woman who he or she is. I think people are always afraid of what they don't understand or what they fear. I can respect someone who says, "I don't understand it, and the idea scares me." I think that is fair and logical, if you can take that approach. However, choosing to hate or dismiss someone's identity and thoughts based solely on your fear and ignorance makes you part of the problem.

Listen, there will always be moments where you will make snapped, rushed, or emotional decisions. However, you have to take a moment to separate yourself from your own individual biases and look at the big picture. Sometimes you will end up with the same conclusions, but at a minimum you will have more respect for the other side. In a world with so much pain from things we cannot control, we must show more restraint in passing judgment. We must show more compassion in how we judge others and their beliefs and actions. We all are different, but that is our strength and we have to embrace that concept. So the next time you find yourself in opposition to someone's beliefs just take moment to pause and think to yourself, "What would I do in that person's shoes?"

Politics

Eleven score and thirteen years ago, our founding fathers laid the foundation of what would become the bedrock of a strong country. In channeling my inner Abe Lincoln, I can't help but wonder what he and our forefathers would think of America the Great now. I would dare to think they wouldn't see anything great about our country at the moment. Look, I don't go pointing the fingers at who is wrong and who is right. However, it is pretty clear to a trained, nonbiased eye that everyone is playing a part in our country's demise. Let's go back a few years and look at where American politics went wrong.

First, let me give the disclaimer of political affiliations in saying that I am a registered Republican. However, I only vote Republican in local/city elections. I tend to lean Democratic in national races but never oppose crossing the aisle in voting. As someone who has voted for Clinton, Bush, Kerry, Obama, Romney, and soon a different Clinton, I can say with confidence that I am open-minded and not afraid to be different. I have come to understand that if you take titles and faces out of the argument of political issues, most people can work together for a solution. However, people today become so enraged with their political hatred of the other side that they fail to see the big picture. People tend to have more loyalty to their political party than their country. In some cases they have more loyalty to their party than to their own God. I am no historian, but I really feel like our great country is at a crossroads. I believe where we are as a country comes from many of our elected leaders being practically worthless and our citizens being out of touch with the truth.

The first example is fairly obvious, as we have career politicians who spend decades in office and never do anything constructive beyond collecting a check. When it comes down to the people, the answers get a little harder to understand. First, let's take an honest look at the last two presidents, George W. Bush and Barack Obama. W was such an epic failure as president, and he was elected twice with everyone knowing his vice president was really in charge. Then comes a junior senator from Illinois to fix the failures of the Bush administration. Everyone across the aisle on day one decided they were not going to listen to anything this man had to say. I remember one senator going so far as to say Obama was a one-term president, and he would not support him on anything. I even remember once Obama found a package of money-tree seeds and wanted to plant them for every American, but his Republican friends in congress didn't want to vote for it because it was a bad idea. I'm joking, of course, but there were times it felt like no matter what he did, the votes were always on party lines, and that should never happen. Of course, there will be times where certain core principles will divide people, but to always discount a president or leader is never productive. After years and years of this political version of *Mean Girls*, we have a divided country.

I've always tried to separate people from their political ideology, as I know there are many who become passionate about their beliefs. One night I was sitting at a bar overhearing this guy give praise to a certain Republican candidate who once was a reality-television star. After listening through a few drinks and biting my tongue to the point I left a mark, I turned to this gentleman and asked him one very simple question: "Excuse me, sir, I'm thinking about voting for Trump. Can you help me by explaining his positions on foreign policy, the military, education, health care, and social security?" The gentleman looked at me dumbfounded and quite confused by my question. I responded by saying, "Well, I figure those areas are the biggest areas of government spending, and I would like to know his plans."

Again, he looked quite confused and maybe a little frustrated that I had asked him a question like that at all. After he fumbled around looking for something smart to say, I stopped him and said, "I don't mean any disrespect"—even though I did—"but I find it hard to believe you would give your vote to someone who hasn't given one clear vision of his plan for our country." I continued by saying, "That's the problem with our country—we give our votes to candidates without them earning them." I recommended that he learn more about his candidate and give his vote based on the facts, not the hatred for the other party's candidate. Sure, neither choice is ideal, but for me the choice isn't remotely close. That being said, if we really want productive change, we must make our politicians accountable for their actions and words.

The common thread we share, no matter our race, religion, background, or sexual preference, is that we are Americans. We must remember that and start looking for the greater good in each situation instead of placing blame on people and groups. This country will only be as strong as its weakest link, so until we stop ignoring the needs of the people who need help the most, we will have deep divisions that will tear us apart. My hopes and dreams for our country revolve around the simple idea of government of the people, by the people, for the people. Thank you, Mr. Lincoln.

Dream Girl

I've always said love is for the lucky. I could have never guessed that after years and years of searching for Miss Right, she would show up right in front of me. Normally it's hard for me to talk to beautiful women in random places. I've never been that comfortable just walking up and introducing myself. A million things go through my head before I speak, and none are her saying, "Yes, here's my number." This night was different, and when she walked through the door of this restaurant, everything seemed perfect in that moment. I'm sure the moon was full and the stars were all in alignment. There was glow around her, and for that moment her halo was so bright there was no one else was in the room but me and her. As she walked toward me, she smiled as if to say, "I see you there, handsome." I smiled back and gave her the only sexy face I know—the look that says, "I see you, beautiful, and yes, you are my future, so come over and let me buy you a drink." Guess she didn't see my look, 'cause she walked right past me and disappeared in the darkness.

I turned back to my drink, but it didn't have the same taste, as my mind was solely on this mysterious woman who just passed me. I looked ahead so I didn't look like I was searching for her. However, I've been searching for her for my entire adult life. She was perfect in every way, and I wanted to know her more than ever. I put my empty glass down and flagged the bartender for more liquid courage. Right at that moment, a voice came from behind me: "Hey you, what are you drinking?" It was her, and every cool bone in my body was broken—what I said next, I'm not so sure. I'm sure my lips were moving and words came out, but I'm sure it wasn't very sexy. But even with me standing there crippled by her beauty, she laughed and smiled. The conversation was very friendly and sincere, as if she were my lifelong best friend.

We sat talking and drinking for hours, totally forgetting there were other people around. We talked politics, vacation spots, sports, and even *Star Trek* versus *Star Wars*. This was truly my soul mate, and nothing in the stars could tell me differently. Everything from when she first walked through the door to that point was perfection and beauty. I knew the moment I saw her face that this night was life changing. If we had been in Vegas, I would have been looking for a chapel so I could make her my wife. Maybe we would have had a *Shaft* wedding like Will and Lisa on *Fresh Prince of Bel-Air*. It was that serious, and all I could think about as I closed our tabs was what was next. What came next is not for the young and restless but for the mature and hopeless romantics.

We stood in the parking lot and continued our conversation for what seemed like hours. I stood over her, lost in her smile and dreaming about tasting her lips, tasting her body, and feeling her skin on my skin. She grabbed my hand, interweaving her fingers with mine. I placed my hand on her cheek and leaned in to kiss gently her on the forehead. Her eyes closed, and she exhaled with a smile of endearment and lust. Her lips were perfectly moist with a slight sheer of pink lipstick, and they begged to be kissed. I leaned in and kissed her lips, but this kiss was so different from any I'd had before. Yes, her lips were soft, and kisses were passionate with love. However, this kiss opened up a piece of her I had never experienced; I kissed her body and tasted her soul, a soul meant for me and only me. A body and soul nothing short of a gift from the gods. We made our way into her car, with her in the driver's seat and me just a passenger, having lost my sense of time and place. She asked if I wanted to follow her home, and yes, I agreed. I got out of her car and into mine and followed her to her house.

I listened to some random mix of Drake songs as I followed her, thinking of what was going to happen next. In the background Drake sang, "I got my eyes on you; you're everything that I see. I want your hot love and emotion. I can't get over you; you left your mark on me. Just hold on; we're going home. Just hold on; we're going home." I was so excited, and all the blood was rushing to only one part of my body. I got out of the car and adjusted my pants to hide my excitement, pulling Mr. Happy up and tightening my belt over him to hide my pure excitement for this moment. I met her at her car, opened her door, and reached for her hand. I guided her out, and she stood in front of me. Perfection as the moonlight twinkled in her eye and her smile invited me to kiss her with my earlier passion. I held her hand with one hand and placed my other in the small of her back. I pulled her close to me and held her so close I knew she had to feel my excitement through my pants.

We ventured inside, my lips never leaving her body. We bypassed the bedroom and chose the sofa to discover each other's bodies. I placed her on the sofa in a seated position and stood over her to catch my breath and tell her how beautiful she was. I placed my body between her legs, lightly grinding her body as I gently kissed her down her face, taking the occasional moment to lick and bite her between kisses. Her eyes closed, and her hands grabbed my back with passion and love. I slid down to my knees and unbuttoned her jeans, pulling her pants and pink undies off and laying them to the side. Dinner was light, and now it was time for dessert. This was my moment to prove to her this wasn't a fling. This wasn't some random encounter, but the perfect night that only the gods could have made possible. I tasted her, I touched her, I kissed her, I injected my tongue inside her and made love to her with my tongue. She grabbed my head and squeezed it while screaming my name and cursing the heavens. This was my pleasure to make her feel good in this moment. She tried to pull away as she climaxed, but I wanted all of her and wanted to taste the moment. Her moans of pleasures became louder, and her grip was more intense. As she trembled from the climactic finish of my oral pleasure bomb, she pulled me close and kissed my ear, then whispered, "I want you now and forever." I turned to look her in the eyes and said, "I will never leave your side. Give me all of you, and you can have all of me."

She stood up and led me upstairs to her bedroom. She took off the rest of her clothes as she walked toward the room, leaving a trail of lust and clothes. I followed suit, reached the bedroom at full attention, and joined her in bed. We wrestled in the bed, kissing and exploring as if we were teenage kids rushing before our parents got home. We were lost in the moment with not a care in the world, as the only thing that mattered was our love. She showed me her heart, and she showed me that I would never need another woman but her. She put me on my back, kissing my lips and exploring my body with her hands. She lay on top of me, pressing her breasts against my chest and slowly sliding down, kissing all pressure points. I'll spare you the details of her skills with hands and tongue, but never have I felt so good.

I'd been with plenty of other women, but none had ever felt so right. None had ever felt as if they were my perfect match. Her kisses, her moans, even the sweat that ran down her chest was perfect and felt so good. We played this love game all night and never lost the lust of the moment. Every man looks for that special person to light his world. She was my sun to light my day and my moon to light my night. This wasn't just about sex, good conversation, or even some delusional one-night stand. This was the atomic connection of two souls crashing at the right time to form a bright explosion of emotion and love. We lay there, gently rubbing and caressing each other, and we didn't have to speak because I already knew what she was thinking. She smiled and looked at me, knowing that she was safe and protected forever and a day in my arms. We lay there holding each other as the sun came up.

This was the conclusion of a perfect day, a perfect encounter, a perfect moment of lust, love, and emotion. I was in love and knew my search for the perfect woman was over. No more first dates, no more catfish experiences with app dating, and no going to bed alone without the warmth of knowing someone loves me. We lay there and fell asleep with the soundtrack of our night playing in our heads and in our dreams. I woke up the next day with the biggest smile on my face, staring at the ceiling and grinning ear to ear just like a Cheshire cat. I took a moment to laugh at myself and one lonely tear fell from my eye. Why? Because I realized that last night, I had met the woman I had prayed for, the woman I had wished and searched for since I was a little boy. My dream girl! The woman I know is perfect for me and I will never lose love for and will always have my heart was truly my dream girl.

I turned to my right to find myself alone in my bed with the memory of the best dream I had ever had. I had a brief pity party, but once I put my feet on the floor, I realized that the heavens had blessed me with a vision of what true love is and how it should feel. For that I am thankful, and I have hope that Miss Right is real and I will find her one day. So, my dream girl, I am leaving for work now, but I will see you later tonight in my dreams. I love you.

Friendship

Am I my brother's keeper? Yes, I am, says G-Money right before Nino shoots and kills him in the classic movie *New Jack City*. Not how you thought I would start a thought on friendship? Over the years I have seen a lot of people come and go in my life, but one thing I always try to keep consistent is my core group of friends. I've always tried to be the friend that is there any time someone calls. However, lately in life I've seen things become a little one-sided in the friendship department. Of course, I have friends that I don't have to see or talk with every day, but even on the best of days, it helps to know that somewhere in the world, someone is thinking of you enough just to say, "Hello, how are you?" As we grow older, many of our relationships change, and we are forced to adjust our circle of friends to meet where we are in life. When I was younger, it was always me and guys out looking for the ladies. Now all the guys are married, and I'm pretty much the only single friend left to hit the bar scene. My friends are single women, and guy time is cut to a minimum. Guess this is just a stage of life we must all go through to figure out who is important and who is not.

As in any relationship, professional, friendly, or even romantic, you just want to be appreciated. You just want to receive what you give in loyalty, respect, and friendship. There should be only one rule in friendship, and that's to always have my back. Male or female, there shouldn't be anything selfish about friendship, and you always treat others with the respect you want in return. I've seen too many friendships become one-sided, and people will take advantage of situations and people with kind hearts. There are always signs, and you must view them and take them seriously, or you will find yourself hurt by someone you trust. Someone told me once that I don't trust people when I should. I kindly corrected them and told them it's quite the opposite. I wholeheartedly trust the people I let in my life and will do so until they give me a reason not to. I will be there any way I can, whether I've known the person thirty years or thirty days. That's just how I am, and I wish more people would do the same. However, I'm not big on second chances, as I feel people are who they will always be. If someone fails to see the value in your friendship and walks away, why shouldn't I do the same? Don't get me wrong, I will miss and mourn the good times we shared as friends. However, I cannot allow someone to push me aside anytime they feel the need to.

I remember a close friend of mine, someone I considered a brother, allowed our friendship to change over something I viewed as petty. His wife was sick, and they were really having a hard time with the emotions of going through this illness. I understood and respected their privacy, but this is my brother, and I wanted to be there for him and his family, even if it was just stopping by with food or to say hello and let her know I was thinking about her. Every time I asked to stop by, I was told I couldn't. However, with everyone posting their activities on social media, I would see people stopping by to see them all the time. People who didn't even live in the state, who had known them for a fraction of the time I had known them, were allowed to stop by and say hello, but I couldn't. Sure, it's petty, but I think everyone makes decisions for a reason. They might not tell their reasons, but there is always a reason for the things we do.

Another friendship came as a pleasant surprise but ended once she started dating someone. Here one day, gone the next—all because we just couldn't see eye to eye on her relationship. Deep down I understand the layers of fairness and know there is some blame on my end as well. However, I firmly believe that true friendship begins and ends with open and honest communication. If someone is willing to eject me without thought or hesitation, it's hard to imagine we were ever friends to begin with. I will not change my methods of engaging with people based on my perception of being treated unfairly. I wholeheartedly believe that most people still respect loyalty, kindness, and friendship, but I must admit it becomes harder and harder as the days pass.

Music

"The perfect verse over a tight beat" is one of my favorite lines from a movie. It just speaks to me in a unique way. It takes me back to the days of rushing to be the first in line to buy a new album at the music store. My teachers knew I wouldn't be in class on Tuesday mornings because I had to get the latest release before everyone else. Walking through the halls with my headphones, jamming out to the newest music from my favorite artist—those were the days where I couldn't wait to crack open the CD case to view the book and see who produced and wrote each song. I remember my very first album like it was yesterday—Supersonic by J. J. Fad! Even all these years later I can recite the lyrics like I did when I was a kid: "The *S* is for super, the *U* is for unique, the *P* is for perfection!" Hey, don't judge me; I'm pretty sure most of you know the words, too.

There was something about music during that time period that was very honest and very pure. It crossed all genres of music from hip-hop to rock and roll. I think of all the subgenres that came from this era of music. Groups like Nirvana, Wu-Tang, and Third Eye Blind made music that will never be lost to time. Today is such a different story, as many groups make songs only for financial success without a true love for their craft.

See, I believe that the early 1990s to the mid-2000s was truly one of the renaissance periods for music. I remember someone told me once that music was like McDonald's. When you are young, you love the idea of McDonald's, but as you age and mature your choice in food changes. Your taste buds mature, and you desire things beyond a burger and fries. At the time I thought they had a point, until I realized McDonald's was bad for you then and is still bad for you now. Sure, your tastes may change, but that doesn't make something good when it is not. I listen to today's music and can't help but yearn for the days of '90s R and B. The realness of '90s New York hip-hop and the flavor of southern rap in the decade after 2000. I miss the authentic rhythms from groups like Counting Crows, Linkin Park, and Wu-Tang to name a few.

There is still good music being made, but unfortunately there isn't much for today's generation to be proud of. Music is supposed to connect us to the rhythm of the people, and I must say today's rhythm is off beat and lacks substance. It's just blah, blah, blah; trap, trap, trap; hook, hook, hook on a nice beat. I need some gravy with my biscuits to keep everything together. Maybe I'm getting old and just prefer the gentle melodies of NPR.

Random One

When you are writing your first book, many thoughts go through your head. Will people like it, will they understand it, and will you remember everything you wanted to say? There is a certain tone that you want reach in touching your readers. For me that tone is all about finding a common thread of positivity in all subjects. I'm a firm believer that there is a silver lining in all situations. Yes, there will be times you have to search hard to find it, but you have to be on the lookout for it. Most things we do in life are about finding some level of happiness. However, many tend to ignore the tiny blessings we receive every day.

Happiness is in the details of our actions. It can come from the simplest of actions that make us happy without us even thinking about it. Some will find joy in sitting down in a comfy chair after a long day. Maybe it's the aroma of Starbucks coffee in the morning minus the long wait in line, of course. For me it's a big spoonful of Cinnamon Toast Crunch in the morning. It's finding a couple of extra fries at the bottom of a bag of fast food. It's the first gulp of beer on a summer's day. See, happiness is always in the details of things that we do daily, and we tend to ignore those things. Cherish these moments and view them for what they are: blessings. Find what makes you happy, and never let it go.

Failure

I have failed all types of ways in my life. I've failed as a businessman, a friend, a boyfriend, a son, and even a father. In all my failures, I've always tried to look at those situations and ask, "What could I have done better?" I've asked, "What could I have done differently to have received a different result and prevent failure?" That being said, it is those failures that have shaped my path to the man I am today. I think of a time when my life was crumbling before me. Love life was a disaster. My friends and family were completely in the dark about my emotional distress. My businesses were all on the brink of shutting down. Those were some dark and endless days where nothing was good or going my way. I remember lying in my bed and thinking of the different ways to kill myself. I thought pills, I thought a gun shot, I even dreamed of just walking into the ocean and swimming until I couldn't swim anymore.

When things are not going well, your failures become very obvious and more painful. Where are your friends and family to save you from yourself? Where are all the "Let's be friends" when things get dark and you have nowhere to turn? Guess the beauty of struggle is that it gives you perspective on who is really friend, foe, or fake. You begin to question who is really family or stranger. Things become clear in your darkest hour if you are paying attention. Yes, you failed; yes, you may be a failure in that moment in time. However, no failure should prevent you from trying again. There is a silver lining to everything we do in life.

I remember lying there in my bed seeing my life replay in my dreams. I saw the mistakes, I saw the people I loved, and I saw the people who said they loved me. I saw the people whom I'd loved and lost. I saw the supporters, and I saw the haters who never had my back or front. What became very clear to me at that dark hour was that failure did not define me. In each of my failures, I was able to bounce back toward another venture. Whether it was me, fate, God, or something I do not understand, I was provided a second chance. Bottom line, I had to choose to lie in bed and continue to feel the pain of yesterday, or feed the spark of the blessings provided in a new day.

It's simple, no matter how low or high yesterday was to you. Wake up and be better than yesterday, as tomorrow is not a promise. Wake up and continue to dream of better days for yourself and the people around you. I know the heartache can get you down, and you want to walk away from the world, but you have to always shine. We all have this spark or glow inside us, and failure can be like big splash of water that puts it out. However, nothing should ever take our glow from us, as we have to always find a way to shine. Find the light bringers, the magic makers, and the world shifters to challenge you. These game changers are the people you let in your life to break you open and uplift your spirit. Letting our failures define who we are and take away our glow will never solve the problem. The answer is always inside of us, and mostly it says to keep pushing and never give up. You can achieve any and everything, even through failure. Just never forget to learn, and never make the same mistake twice.

Soul Mate or Mistake

I've always found it amazing how people choose who they date, especially when it comes to women choosing a man. See, men couldn't care less about whom we date. Don't get me wrong, all men have standards and individual preferences. However, most men's standards are pretty petty compared with women's standards. A man might think does she cook, clean, look good, and have the type of curves he desires? Take online dating, for example, to see how people make a choice. A man logs into the site and uploads his best pictures—a couple of selfies, a couple of pet pics, and the famous me-and-the-guys picture. A woman will post similar, but her pictures will be of her wearing her biggest smile. There's a dirty secret that many don't want to admit, but most only sign up for the possibly of sex.

Don't get me wrong; I'm sure there are some good men and women who have noble intentions. Unfortunately, the majority only care about one thing: hooking up! For a man it is easy to throw up a couple of pictures, send out dozens of feelers, and see what happens. Even if only 10 percent of the women reply, there is almost 100 percent chance you will get a date with someone. From there it comes down to if you are at least half of what you present online. Once you pass the "He's not crazy" and "He looks like his pictures" test, you have a strong chance of having sex with an online match. Many men understand these odds and are willing to play the craps table of love.

I'm sure there is a reader saying, "I met a guy online, and he is wonderful." Again, this isn't one size fits all, and I'm sure he may be good, but that doesn't change the reality of how you met and his motivation for wanting to meet you. He signed up for the app or site for the sole reason to meet a girl to have sex with him. In some cases, many women will say, "That's cool, because I signed up for the same reason." I applaud those women and have tons of respect for you. However, do not be fooled into believing that his attraction to you is nothing more than what he saw in your profile pic. So again, how do we pick a partner today? Is it based on physical attraction, wealth, or common interest? Maybe it's out of desperation or the timing of your life at that current moment. Some even go as far to say they are in search of their soul mate.

That has always been an interesting subject for me, as I'm not sure there is such a thing. By definition, a soul mate is someone who was placed on this earth just for you. Well, what if my soul mate was born in Brazil, and I never go to Brazil—am I to miss out on true love? My belief is that a soul mate is a combination of all the experience you have had in dating wrapped into one person. For starters, a soul mate will be your friend first and foremost, as you will connect on the same experiences. You will have many of the same likes and dislikes. The similarities of your life give you the ability to relate to each other where others have failed. If you are picking a person based on a look, smile, or just one good date, you are setting yourself up for failure. Give your heart to someone who earns it, not to someone who takes it just because you offered it. Never trust a big butt and a big smile—they might be poison to your long-term plans. Pick wisely!

Dating

I've been on what feel like a thousand dates in my life. I'm fairly sure I am the king of first dates. I've dated women from all backgrounds, black, white, Asian, Latino, rich, poor, short, and tall. I'm even sure one of those Tinder dates was from another planet. So it's pretty safe to say I've dated and done it all. One thing I have learned from each encounter is that we are all unsure of what we really want in a mate. Of course, we have an idea, but it is only an idea, and most likely a bad one. In my mind, I can see my dream girl. She is so clear and visual I can even tell you her horoscope. I know her background, her professional life, her physical attributes, and even how she makes love. She is a vision, crystal clear, but at the end of the day, she is but a dream.

Yes, I do believe dreams come true, but even the best dream has missing parts. Those missing parts are not for us to fill in the blanks with our own ideas. This is not an argument for a "beauty and the beast" type of love for those who think that's where I am going. I'm only saying sometimes our standards are too high, and we ignore the potential of greatness and happiness when it is right in front of our eyes. Sure, I want my future partner to be beautiful and rich, and make love like a professional. Like a professional, not actually being a professional, of course. That being said, it is up to me to define what "beautiful," "rich," and "good lover" mean. I cannot put my own prejudices on the people I meet and share a moment with. No one can ever live up to the greatness of a dream or vision. We can only hope that someone thinks enough of us to be willing to learn and discover things together.

It is through this discovery process that we can look inside a person and see more than the outer self. We can see the inside of the soul, and in that soul you may see your dream. I've thought about all the women I judged so harshly because I walked into a date wanting them to be something they were not. Not even taking a moment to actually listen to what they had to offer. Not paying attention to what made them special as people, as people who took the time to sit down with me. I think of all the women who did the same to me—not taking the time to listen to what I had to say and offer, but listening for what they wanted to hear and what they wanted me to do for them.

I believe that if we pay attention to our surroundings, we can see the truth in everyone's actions and intentions. We will see the girl who thought you were handsome and gets butterflies when you walk into a room. You can see the guy who is your friend but dreams about making you happy in ways beyond friendship. If we pay attention, we wouldn't have to waste time chopping through weeds. If we open our eyes, the crystal-clear dream could be standing right in front of us, hoping for the chance to proudly stand by your side.

Getting Over Someone

There comes a time where you find yourself heartbroken from losing a person you care about. Loss comes in many forms: death, relocation, self-growth, betrayal, and thousands of others. However, none hurts quite as bad as when you lose someone you love, and you don't know why—you walk away from a person, but you are not sure why you decided to part ways. Was it something that person heard about you? Was it something you did or didn't do? All you know is that one day someone very important to you is no longer a part of your life. This pill is hard to swallow for even the strongest of people, and there is no clear solution to stop the pain.

Recently, I have had to deal with heartbreak. It was the worst kind, as I not only lost a friend but I lost someone I loved. This story starts no different than most love stories. Guy meets a girl and becomes infatuated with her style, beauty, and grace. However, in this situation, the girl the guy ends up falling for isn't the girl he first meets. This guy, my dumb self, falls for her equally stylish, beautiful, and graceful sister. Go figure, sometime Cupid shoots you in the ass and makes an ass out of you in one shot. This wasn't some sinister plot to engage in the ultimate ménage à trois—it was bad timing meets perfect timing. Let me explain what I mean. I first had the honor of meeting Savannah at a charity event for the homeless. She had this rebel, wild child mentality, and I can honestly say I was attracted. She was beautiful in every way imaginable: smart, loyal, fierce in her belief, and easy on the eyes. But for me, I always apply gentleman rules when chasing love. I decided not rush things but take my time and get to know her better.

We traded one-sided messages, meaning I was always the one to begin a conversation no matter the subject. I would ask her out and be kindly rejected, mostly due to scheduling. I believed her. I never felt like I was bothering her, but I did feel I wasn't a priority for her. She was such a free spirit in our conversations and her mystery piqued my interest. That interest came to a hard stop, as Savannah mentioned via social media she was going to go backpacking around Europe for several months. That came as a shock but not a surprise, as her free spirit was something I greatly admired. However, I could not duplicate her eagerness to just leave everything and everyone behind, but we never got to a place where she would ask this of me.

For a moment, I thought she could be someone very special, and maybe I should think about backpacking with her. Funny how timing is always one of the main factors in finding someone special. Meet a cool woman and just like that she is off to see the world with a one-way ticket and no plan to return. This brings me to the other side of the equation. Savannah's loving, friendly, cheerful, flirty, and slightly pessimistic sister, Madison. Madison was at first glance an equally beautiful carbon copy of her sister. However, it didn't take long to see there were major differences between the two. Savannah was solid in her thoughts and beliefs, and Madison was unsure of herself and beliefs. In Madison I could see a person who had been wounded by life and wanted to loved. Although very outgoing and personable, she was a gentle spirit, someone who listened more than talked. She absorbed the energy from her surroundings and fed on it—good energy around her and good energy she gave in return. Bad energy around her, and you might wanna duck, 'cause there's no telling when she might blow. I do mean "blow" as in her letting off steam, not some crazy person.

So, here is where you come to the crossroads of a potentially crazy situation. On one road is a person who is all of the things you are not: adventurous, spontaneous, and full of life. The other road is someone gentle, caring, and loving whose energy compliments your own. Although I was never given a choice by either, I decided for myself to make a choice. That was my mistake, and my heart hates that choice every day. I chose the latter, in wanting a future with Madison. There was no discussion, no sit down and this is what is, just me and you. No, I chose to be arrogant and assume there was no way she couldn't feel the same. I didn't change my approach, as I wanted to explore friendship with her first, never exposing my true feelings or passions. I mean, how can you build a lasting relationship from lust and physical contact? You don't truly love a person until you realize it isn't the sex, the gifts, or the dinners, but just the idea of them not being there. If you can go longer than an hour and not think about someone, then they are not the one.

Madison has never left my mind; even as I write these words she is still in my spirit. Her laugh and clumsiness were all things that I adored. She told me about a time when a man she thought loved her cheated and ended their relationship. I couldn't help but think that guy was a dumb ass, for who cheats on perfection? She was my dream, the perfect person I wanted to spend my entire life exploring, growing with, and loving. Our friendship was the perfect kind of friendship, as we would talk about almost anything and explore different life experiences together. Sometimes she would hug me so strong as if to say, "Please, never leave me." There were times our conversations were so face-to-face I would lean back to not kiss her. She'd give a gentle touch on my thigh to let me know she was there. I would put my hand on the small of her back as I opened the door for her. These were the moments that made us who we were.

If she wasn't by my side, our friends would ask where she was. If I wasn't there, they would ask about me. We had become an item without trying to be, as our friendship was the most valuable thing to us. She was a cool breeze on a hot summer's day, and I wanted nothing more than to feel her gentle spirit around me always. However, like all things that grow and develop, there must be some direction on how to grow. I wanted to spread our relationship beyond the confines of just friendship, as there was so much more we could be. I found those feelings of lust and temptation creep into my thoughts each moment I spent with her. I wanted nothing more than to be by her side and for her to be by mine. She made me a better man, a better person, because I wanted to equal her spirit and her energy.

However, for every road we travel in life, we have to follow our own path. For me that path was clear and solid, filled with a lasting love and friendship. Madison's path was nowhere near mine, going a completely different direction. In hindsight, I might have imagined the whole friendship. The glances from her eyes were not for me. The hugs and smiles were nothing more than brotherly contact. As I dwelled on every little sign, she was in her own world, and I was nothing more than a casual stranger passing by. Random guy at a random moment, maybe that's the title for part two of my book. No, I kid, but once the truth was revealed, she did not see me as I saw her. That's where my heartbreak began and where I became just another random guy. Embarrassed, hurt, and heartbroken, feeling like the biggest loser in the world. My pain didn't come from her not feeling the same. My pain came from her looking at me as if I was so wrong in thinking that was even a possibility. Like that was the worst idea she had ever heard. That's why the pain was so bad—the look she gave me was embedded into my dreams.

How do you move on and get over someone you briefly cared so much about? The sad truth is that you never do get over that person. I know without doubt that I loved her with my soul. She is and will forever be stained on my heart without question. What is a person to do with this type of heartbreak? You wipe away the tears from your face, look into the mirror and say, "Yes, I love her, but somewhere somebody wants to love me." It will be at that moment when you meet that special person—the stars will align, and you will understand your wounds will be healed. I will never forget Madison, and I hope my words reach her and she knows I am sincere. I hope I never lose that yearning desire to share the love in my heart.

Not everything happens for a reason; sometimes we make the wrong decision and have to find a way to deal with the outcome. There are those moments, sitting at the bar alone, that I think of her, and I stop and smile. I am reminded that even though she left my side and chose to love another, even though it has been a long time since I heard her laugh or seen her smile, I will always know that for one brief moment our connection was real, and our paths crossed. Even if she never saw it or felt the same, for me it will always be good enough. That is where I find my peace and my comfort.

Online Dating

I have come to despise the idea of online dating and what it does to relationships. In my humble opinion, online dating is the modern version of the mail-order bride. Seriously, let's think about the concept of online dating in a nondigital way. Of course, it seems cool and easy to meet people by just tapping a button. Just pull your phone out of your pocket and open an app, swipe left or right to find the perfect person to meet. What if the dating game meant you drive to a location on a map, knock on the door, and some creepy old lady greets you and hands you a big yellow-pages-style book with faces of women or men. For those who don't know what the yellow pages are, I encourage you to look that up. I'm sure you'll find some cool memes out there. I digress, but I think you understand my point of turning the pages of a massive book to find someone to date.

There would be several books: the book of Tinder for the quick and easy; the books of eHarmony and Match for those willing to spend a little more; and several smaller books for those not willing to spend top dollar for the best mates. These last books are for the cheap and desperate who don't really put a value on love. After going through thousands of faces, you decide on a friendly face that catches your eye. How many of you would enjoy that process and view your pick with pride? I get that I am generalizing, but this is the root of online dating: flipping through the yellow pages for the perfect person to call. When you search ads for a repairman, how to do you choose? The ad with boldest letters or best overall design, or is it the smile of the person pictured? There are hundreds to pick from, and how can you know who will be best for you? All are trained to do the same job, but who is the best person to help you solve your problem?

That is the fundamental problem with online dating: there is no perfect way to weed out the scum and make a good choice. Sure, you can pick someone and go on a couple of dates to get a feel for each other. But people will lie to get your booty, I mean, business. The repairman wants your business and will say and do anything to get it. A person's main reason for joining a site or app is always simplified to looking for that special person. So how can you tell who is special and who is not? Surely not by a profile pic and a romantic description. I assure you, it's hard to tell even after a couple of dates. In your profile, you have already told the person your type and what you are interested in. At this point, all they have to do is play the game long enough to get what they want from you.

Take my advice, the only way to find someone with substance is by going slow and steady. Get to know a person, become friends, play hard to get. All the subtle things that help a person truly know you inside and out. I was once told you don't truly know someone until four seasons have passed. You need that amount of time to truly see a person's core self. Don't get me wrong, there will always be exceptions to the rule. Even the unlucky can get lucky now and then, but why take the risk? Why place your heart in the hand of a person you don't really know?

Now my next issue is aimed more at ladies, and I'm sure the guys will take some issue here. Many men join dating websites and apps for one reason only: random sexual encounters. Ladies, think back to the last guy you fell head over heels for only to find he wasn't the one. This next example applies to both online dating and dating in general. I just want you to understand how we as men process our emotions. If we meet a woman and we are sexually attracted to her at first contact, that is the only thing we care about, and we won't rest until we've conquered that mountain. A profile page has no substance beyond the superficial remarks like "looking for relationship," "not interested in casual dating," and blah, blah, blah. In reality, when I see those lines in a profile, it's almost pure comedy.

My first and only thought while searching: Is she sex-able? If not, move to the next profile and look for a face that is my type. Ladies, why would you want someone who looks at you solely as a piece a meat? If you don't believe me, ask your online hookup or online boyfriend, "What about my profile did you like?" I guarantee you will get some generic answer like, "I don't know. You were different" or "You stood out. The rest were not my type at all." Again there is no real substance in the process, as it is only designed to spark your sexual interest. So you go on a couple of dates; he's not crazy, and he's easy to talk with, so you let your guard down. He has you right where he wants you, and you give up the booty. There are only a few paths from here: he got what he wanted from you and moves on, or he keeps you around for entertainment without commitment because you are fun and he likes the idea of you. Then the lucky actually decide to try and make things work.

In none of these examples do you truly know the person, and you are still taking a major risk of heartbreak, rejection, or a big case of the crazies. Again apologies for having to generalize, but relationships are not "add, pour, and then serve" instant recipes for success without putting in the work. Real home cooking always tastes better than instant and fast foods. There's no way a man can respect a woman if she makes everything so easy for him. After two dates you give him the cookies, after two weeks you are posting pictures together, and after two months you are changing your profile status to "In a relationship." These are all warning signs for a man, and if he rolls with your actions, then it is a warning sign for the ladies.

It takes four seasons—winter, summer, spring, and fall—to understand how a person will respond to you and how you will respond to him or her. Finding love isn't supposed to be easy, but building a relationship should be easy because you should be in control of the situation. Not allowing some digital idea of a person to becoming your dream and idea of good. So next time you decide to join an app to click or swipe for love, I suggest you grab a phone book and try your luck there. I'm sure the odds are just as good.

Rhythm of Life

There is a rhythm to everything we do in life, everything from mowing the yard to hailing a cab after catching dinner on a busy Friday night. That rhythm guides us toward the success we have in everyday activities. Have you ever noticed that you tend to have better workouts at different times of the day? For me the best time is the early-morning hours before the sun comes up. Then for others it is right after work on the way home. Many are not aware of their daily rhythms, as they live out life not seeing the beauty in the harmony of life. People, opportunities, and life pass right in front of our eyes as we ignore the rhythm of life.

I challenge everyone to think of the things, people, and opportunities you have missed by not opening your eyes to rhythm of your world. We get lost in a "go with the flow" attitude and accept what comes our way without paying attention to beauty in moments. I once missed the business opportunity of a lifetime by ignoring the signs and being lost in the moment. These moments guide our inner rhythm and point us where we go in life.

Have you ever met a person you admire, and instead of following your heart, you overthink things and end up regretting that choice? That a classic example of getting off beat and not following the rhythm so things will happen as they should. Look, we all have to make choices. Some will be good, and others we will regret. However, if we let the rhythm of life guide us, we can find ourselves in situations that teach us to be better. Don't chase after life; allow life to flow to you and just ride the rhythm. I promise you will not regret it.

Parenthood

There is nothing like the joys of fatherhood. For a brief moment in my life, I was a proud father of one of the most beautiful little girls in the whole wide world. I will spare all the details, as that story will be told on another random day. Yes, there will be a part two, and yes, that was a shameless plug.

Fatherhood gives a man purpose and energy to take on the world for the betterment of his child. He knows that when he leaves the house, he has to provide a safe and productive home for his family. There shouldn't be anything more special to the heart of man than the love from his family. The love of his children can push him in ways he never knew existed. I remember living for the small moments of seeing my daughter's face as she tried new things she hadn't done before. The conversations we had after I picked her from school are memories I never want to forget.

I know a lot of good fathers and have been blessed with memories of calling someone my daughter. I say with a lot of love in my heart to all men of all backgrounds, please always love and care for your family. Never run from your responsibility to be a father to your children, no matter the situation. Children need that strong, dedicated love only a father can give. This is not a knock on single mothers, as I know many who are stronger and more capable than many men. This is just to say that men have a part to play, and we should all embrace the beauty and blessings of being called Father.

So if you have children, tell them that you love them every day, because with any luck, they will wake up one day and actually believe you. If you are blessed to be a father, hug your kids often and share your knowledge so that they will know just how much you love them. That love won't always be returned as they grow and mature, but you will leave an impression on them that will never leave. Children are the best blessing any of us can ever have—treasure them and never let go.

All Human Life Matters

Black lives matter. Blue lives matter. Wait, all lives matter, right? I'm pretty sure gorilla lives matter, too. Yes, that's it—alien ant lives matter. I'm so confused when I listen to the mixed messages about who is important and who isn't. Before I dive into this highly sensitive and political subject, let me say I get the argument from all sides. The biggest problem with this debate is that no side is being honest about their true feelings. I'm sure there are going to be some who read this and say I'm overlooking certain wrongs or oversimplifying. I say that argument is selling each side's hypocrisy short.

Let's have a real conversation about race in the easiest way possible. In every respectable religion on the earth, it is universally believed that God created humans. Science says we are all products of the big bang and evolution. I bring this up to make the point that no matter your belief, it is fairly well accepted that we came from one beginning, thus making us all the same! Now this is where it gets fun. Many would agree that when most human beings die and leave this earth, it is a sad event. This is where the problems and hypocrisy begin on all sides. Before I point fingers, there is a level of generalizing going on here, so bear with me as I make my point. My opinion is based on commentary from many media outlets, social media, network news, everyday commenters, and critics—and from the anger displayed with such passion from certain sides of these issues.

So let me ask a question: If a tree falls in the woods, does it make a sound? I know you are looking at the pages right now and thinking WTF. However, I think this question makes my point very clear. I could ask this question to a thousand people and get different yet similar answers. Some would say it makes a sound, but there's no one around to hear it. Some might dare to say it doesn't make a sound if no one heard it. But whether or not the tree made a sound, the tree still fell.

Now let's ask a different question: If a man dies in the middle of the street, would his death make a sound? We need to divide and conquer to solve this question. The quick and easy answer is no different than if it was a tree falling. What if I told you the man was black? What if I told you he was white? What if I told you he was a cop? What if I told you he was a black homosexual Irish Catholic cop? I'm sure if we ask this question to people of different backgrounds, the answers would vary.

Let's try to take a moment and understand how all people lie about their emotions. The true answer is simple: if a man, no matter his background, dies in the street, we should hear a sound of sadness. If that man was black, there are people who wouldn't care about him or his life. They will ignore why he died and not even consider how he lived. There are those who will pay more attention to how he died than how he lived and make a ton of noise about how he died. If that man was a cop or a white man, there will be those who couldn't care less about how he died or lived. The answer lies in how you relate to the person who died. If you are black and see another black person killed by a person of a different race, you might have a reaction of frustration and pain because that's what you relate to. If you see a white man killed in the line of duty by someone of different race, you might have a reaction of hate and frustration because that's what you relate to.

It's simple to me. I've never seen a group riot and protest over same-race violence. Each side only seems to draw these racial lines when it comes to violence between races. When a white man is killed by police in a questionable manner, where are the protests and cries for justice? When a black cop is killed in the line of duty by someone white, where are the parades and week-long commentary about crime by white folks?

The bottom line is that on some level, many of us have prejudice that we ignore and are afraid to confront. To say it plainly, each racial side has moments that are equally as racist. To be fair, I think Black Lives Matter has a valid point in its criticisms of police, but it has to be fair across the board. The All Lives Matter and Blue Lives Matter folks have a point, but they have to be fair as well and show the same support no matter the skin color of who dies. Our country has deep-seated problems that stem back to our founding fathers. We cannot get past these problems until we start being honest about and realistic about our current state of affairs. The real truth is that we are all shadows and dust only to be lost with the winds of time, and to make ourselves more is just dishonest. My slogan is simple—All Lives End—but how we live our lives is the only thing that matters.

We should always stand up for justice and fairness, but we must fight against our greater evils of trying to separate God's greatest creation by race or disagreement. When a man dies in the street, we shouldn't hear only the sadness and anger of how he died. We should also hear the celebration of how he lived his life and how people loved and cared for him. So don't pass judgment on the situation, as it is not important. What is important is someone is not going home to their family, and all people of all races should feel some sadness in that fact. So in my best Forrest Gump voice, "That's all I have to say about that." Peace and love.

Friends Before Lovers

I have a fundamental belief that has caused me a fair share of heartbreak: friends before lovers. I know some would say that is very old-fashioned and slightly naïve. However, I think I have history to back my beliefs. I know that I am generalizing, but marriages and relationships seemed to last longer in the decades of my parents' generation. I remember my grandmother speaking of young people "courting"—the equivalent of modern-day dating, but which took more time with more rules.

Today, as a man, my expectations once I meet someone are that we will have sex within a week's time. If I'm truly honest with myself, I expect sex after dinner and a movie. The question I have to ask is: Is this a man problem or a woman problem? As a man, am I too aggressive in wanting to have sex with every woman who smiles at me? Are women too eager to have sex with every man who shows them a little attention? Look, I am not making an argument for people not to be open with their sexuality. I'm just saying that when it comes to building strong, long-lasting relationships, sex gets in the way. I believe that if you see someone as a life partner or someone who you want to be exclusive with, sex should be the last piece of the relationship equation. I believe this because if we are truly honest about it, sex is just sex unless there are some real emotions and feelings behind it. Of course, there is such a thing as good sex, but most of the time it doesn't matter because the results are the same, at least for men—sex is just sex, and we are not that picky about who we have sex with most of time.

If you start a relationship on the grounds of sexual intercourse, no matter how strong or good the sexual connection is, failure is a strong probability. Call me a hopeless romantic, but I just know that if you can connect on levels of friendship, energy, and spirituality, your chances of a successful relationship will increase dramatically. Don't believe me? Go back and think of how many times you felt something for someone after a sexual connection only to see those feelings fade. They fade after you get to know the person better, and they fade after you start seeing flaws. Then the sex becomes boring to each side, because they have grown bored with each other. From there you end up in a dead-end relationship with no connection and no spiritual growth.

Of course, there are and will be exceptions to this thought, but overall I'm sure I'm right. I don't believe in a magic number of days when you can finally lie down with someone. When the time is right, I strongly believe the connection will always allow both parties to know. Remember, you don't truly know a person until you have spent four seasons together. Build your relationship on the love of the person, not the lust of a random sexual moment.

Life

Life can be such a roller coaster. Standing in line waiting for the fun to begin, slowly moving forward one step at a time. Each step forward feels like you are still a lifetime away from enjoying the pleasure of the ride. Once you are finally able to get on the ride, it's up and down, fast then slow, and just like that it's over, and you are back in line, hoping to do it all over again. While we are standing in the line of life, it is easy to lose focus and forget about the things that matter. We worry about things we can't control, like the length of the line to get on the ride. The line is the line, and it can't be changed. All you can do is take your time and enjoy the process to get where you are going.

Many things can happen while you wait. Someone can get sick, causing the line to back up. The ride can shut down temporarily, bringing the line to a complete stop. But one thing is for sure: you will get a chance to ride. Then just like that you are on the ride, and it is over. So pay attention to the process; pay attention to the things happening around. The ride is the ride, and it is very predictable. The ride comes, it goes up, and it goes down. It will go fast, and it will slow down. You will feel excited and rushed; then you will feel the calm and the regret. When all is said and done, you will have to get back in line for another ride. So find value in the conversations while waiting your turn. Find enjoyment in the people waiting to feel the thrill with you. Be thankful you even have the chance to get on this ride, because there are many who didn't meet the height requirement. Bottom line? Life is a roller coaster, and it goes by too fast! Enjoy it!

Chance and Opportunity

When I was a teenager, I was given an IQ test to see where I was compared to my peers in school. The results said my IQ was in the 170 range, which put me among the brightest minds not only in my school but in the world. Once I found out my score neared Einstein's, talk about excitement. I never saw myself as a supersmart student. I came from a neighborhood where the first thought was never academics; it was survival. I always felt that I had more street smarts than book smarts. So I couldn't help but wonder what gives us our ability to make wise and smart decisions in life.

In my youth, I never saw value in my daily surroundings and was always envious of my peers. This is not to say I grew up poor. I just looked around and always wanted more than what was afforded to me. I remember waking up early and having to take the bus across town to attend school, but my peers of a different race could just walk to school. We would ride past them and their bigger houses as we pulled up to the school. I guess something inside of me just wanted what they had. Can jealously be a good thing if it motivates you to want more for yourself and life? During those moments in life, I grew up caring only about material things such as clothes, cars, and houses. All I knew at this point was that I had the IQ to help me get where I wanted to be. I was going to step out and do things my way, and no one could stop me.

Shortly after college I started a business with the help of friends and family. Against all odds, I took on the world entrepreneurship, and as a young man I was winning. I was blessed to have everything roll my way for several years. Then BOOM, out of nowhere, I hit the bottom. I don't just mean the bottom; I mean someone hit the bottom and starting digging a special hole just for me. There was nothing I could get right during these times. When I think back to those days, I still don't know how I survived. Where was my worldly brain to help me navigate these troubled waters and times? Then one day it hit me like ton of bricks: sometimes it just doesn't matter how smart you are; it's all about chance and opportunity. Chance is something that is given, but mostly it is something that is made. You have to give yourself the chance to be great, the chance to allow great things to happen to you. If all you do is sit around and talk about what you want to happen, you are missing out on the chance have your dreams come true.

Opportunities come to us almost daily, and many times we fail to see them. The opportunity to meet the right person at the right time. The opportunity to step up and take a chance on yourself. It took me a massive failure to understand that those feelings of envy and jealously were not those things at all. They were nothing more than chance and opportunity giving me the drive to do great things. It doesn't matter how rich you are or how smart you are; at the end of the day, you have to really want it. You have to wake up each day and gamble on your own success.

Give yourself the chance to be great in all phases of your life. Wake up and seek the opportunities that can help you learn and grow as a person. We all are little pieces of art just needing to be molded into a masterpiece. Never stop believing in yourself, never stop dreaming, my friends.

Happiness

They say happiness is a state of mind. I say happiness is a state of heart and soul. The mind can be fooled, but the heart always knows the truth, and the soul always feels it. This is why we must be aware of the people and things we keep in our life. People can steal your joy and rob you of your happiness without you even knowing it. But if you focus your mind, body, and spirit on the joys of life without dwelling on the negative, you can find happiness in everything you do.

If you are miserable, having a bad day, or even depressed, in most cases you are choosing to be in that state. So don't complain about the world and how you are not happy when your happiness is a completely a state of mind. This is not to say bad things don't happen and we are just to ignore everything that doesn't work in our favor. I'm only saying that you have a choice in how long those emotions of sadness should last. If they last longer than a week, you are choosing to stay in a funk. Keep your negativity away from me.

Invisible Man

Misunderstood...underestimated...forgotten. I am the invisible man. Overlooked by those who say they care. In writing my book and reflecting on all the experiences in my life, I see a recurring theme. No matter how much good I try to do, I am almost always the random guy people seem to just forget. I'm no martyr, but I grow frustrated when I give love only to be overlooked in matters of life and love. They doubt my loyalty, they doubt my friendship, they doubt my love, and yet I never stop caring and giving. I am random and not the center of attention, but I always treat others as if they are my center. That has to come with some sort of reward or recognition.

I've loved a few times, and never have I felt I could be someone's number one without strings. Always secondary to others' needs and wants. I'm the guy who is always there for people when they need a friend or shoulder to lean on. I'm the guy who always runs to others when I am needed. I'm the guy people call to get things done. But when I'm in need and I'm hurting on the inside, I'm the guy no one notices.

I have to tackle problems and life by myself because my problems are not important to others. I don't want to sound selfish, but I need comfort from time to time. I want someone to say, "How are you doing?" Like how are you really doing? Is that too much to ask? Even if I'm feeling used from time to time and am overlooked by those I admire and love, I am going to wake up and do my best to help others find a reason to smile.

Foundation

When you build a house, what is one of the first things you do? Lay a foundation, right? What is a foundation made of? Concrete, right? Why not build a foundation with straw, glass, or paper? You don't because they are weak and would cause the house to fall. It makes more sense to build on a strong foundation that can take the weight of the house and weather the storms of rain, snow, and wind. So why do people build relationships on weak and superficial things such as looks, physical attraction, and sex appeal. These things are a factor but should never be the foundation of a relationship.

The best liars are extremely attractive. The best cheats are great in bed. How can you weather the storms of disagreements, agreements, family, and finance on a weak foundation? You may assume it would be easy to build a foundation after you get to know someone. But if you hope to change your foundation after you start your relationship, just like with a house, you have to tear it down and start all over again. So, ladies, before you get caught up in muscles, tattoos, and beards, think of your foundation. Same for the fellas—don't let thick thighs, a thin waist, and a round booty be your main attraction, as these things mean nothing. They fade and go away after the years of time pass. Once a good storm blows through, say good-bye to your relationship house because your foundation is a house of cards, a house built on a superficial foundation rooted in nothing more than hopes and dreams.

Energy

Have you ever walked into a room or a place and got a feeling deep in your gut that something wasn't right? Have you ever met a person and instantly clicked and felt comfortable? What is that feeling? What is the voice telling you to leave or to trust a person? Is it God, Zeus, or a tiny angel on your shoulder telling what to do? I believe it's energy! No silly, not a bolt of lightning or the shock from rubbing your feet on the carpet. It's the internal energy that we give and take during any average day. I like to think of it as the glow. That glow that shines from each of us is our invitation to all the good the world has to offer. See, we can project consciously in any direction or any person once we are fully aware of the energy that we process. However, the absorption of energy is not always a choice. Think of how many times you have been pulled down by someone else's emotions. Someone else's mood or drama that crept into your life and caused you pain. Energy is give-and-take, and we must be aware of the energy that surrounds us.

I'm reminded of a business I owned and how its energy became toxic. Like all businesses, we opened with hopes and dreams of success and riches. However, those feelings went away based on decisions I made. Decisions that cost me friends, family, and relationships, all because I chose to let toxic energy into my life. I hired a young woman who, on the outside, was as beautiful as any woman could be. The inside was a competently different story. Even on introduction there was this force that told me to let her walk away, far away to another planet even. This is not saying she was a bad person, because she was far from that. She was a lovely, kind, and generous person, but she carried tons of baggage from the path she walked. Her only smiles came from alcohol and partying. Her only joy came from money and what it could afford her.

It didn't take people long to see that she was an unhappy person. I'm sure life had not been kind to her, but I always look at every sunrise as a new opportunity, and she viewed every new day as a reminder of pain from the day before. She carried those burdens on her back and shoulders like a semitruck carries cargo. She hated the world and made sure everyone knew how she felt. Her glow, or lack of one, radiated to my staff, to my customers, and even to me. The joy of a new day became the horror of a new nightmare. For months and months, I allowed this hateful and almost evil type of energy to poison my business and my spirit. It forced me to not only close my business but to close myself down in order to cleanse my soul of that dreadfulness.

Even as I write these words, I find myself with little pieces of residue left over from that experience. I wish there were magic glasses we could wear that would show the energy everyone was projecting. Maybe even some bad-energy-protection lotion we could apply daily to block those incoming rays. However, the first step is to be mindful of our own energy. Once we are aware of the power we process internally we can not only change our lives but change the spirit of the world. Imagine a world where people understood the power of "good vibes" projecting good strong positive energy. I am sure the world as we know it would be a much better place. In short, spread love, not hate. Spread love!

Summer Rain

Something about a long summer's rain is almost magical. Rain not only gives us life; it also gives us peace. Beyond the hustle of people moving around doing daily activities, rain seems to stop everyone in their tracks. Every time it rains I take a moment to reflect on the power of the event. How tiny we are in the scheme of the universe. How without that rain we as a people, as a human race, would be nothing. It's the science of the moment; rain falls and rises to fall again. Just like in life, we rise and fall almost daily, but we have to keep going.

This is life, a cycle of flowing rivers of success to great waterfalls of failure, Hurricane-force destruction giving way to reconstruction and growth. Light drizzles of hope increasing to heavy downpours of pain. Water is the blood of our world, and we are but observers of its beauty. A good rain can wash away our fears and pains if we take a moment to marvel in the blessings a good rain can bring. See, there is something about a good rain, as all the answers we seek are found in a simple drop. So the next time you hear on the news of heavy downpours in the area, take a moment, stop, and just enjoy the moment of a good rain.

The Gentleman's Rules?

When did chivalry die? I've heard chivalry is dead so many times I started to wonder, when did it die? I don't think chivalry's demise is quite here, as I do see acts of chivalry almost daily. However, I do believe that chivalry has become less appreciated. I think the reason for that lies somewhere between women wanting to be more independent and simply being used to less chivalrous men. I'm all for an independent woman, as I find it a very attractive trait in a woman. However, I think it is in a man's DNA to take care of his woman in the ways he knows how. Sometimes a woman just needs to let a man do certain things. By certain things, I don't mean revert to being a caveman and drag you down the street by your hair. I'm just saying allow a man to do nice things for you without thinking he has some ulterior motive. As for the guys, stop doing things and having an ulterior motive—you are messing things up for the gentleman's club.

I'm a hopeless romantic, and I believe in things like flowers, gifts, and cards with a message of gratitude. Lately, every time I do something gentlemanly for a woman, I see things turn from "promising" to "what the hell just happened" real fast. She says "You didn't have to do that," or makes that weird face while saying thank you, when "thank you" really means "Why did he do that? I don't like him like that." Then she disappears, leaving me wondering what just happened.

I've actually gotten to the point that if I want to get rid of a woman, I give her flowers. Flowers are the modern-day engagement ring to many ladies, apparently. It's as if giving flowers is making a lifelong commitment, when in reality, flowers are just me saying, "I admire you and want to show you that with a gift. I am thinking of your beauty and wanted prove it."

Little acts of kindness have become not only less appreciated but almost invisible to many ladies. If you do something big and grand, you are being "extra," or my favorite, "thirsty." If you express your emotions verbally then you are doing too much and moving too fast. Unless you match up in the most perfect of ways, you are ignored and overlooked.

I recently found myself admiring a woman, as we were spending a lot of time together. We mutually agreed to take the wait and see what happened, but that never changed how I viewed her. In hindsight I might have waited too long to express my feelings, but I thought my feelings for her were obvious. We always shared these little moments of togetherness, from breakfast to drinks out on the town. One time we stood on her patio looking back at the skyline and discussing the stars in the sky. I wanted more than anything to grab her hand, pull her close, and kiss her. However, the gentleman's rules clearly state you have to take your time and not be aggressive.

I helped her move out of her old house and even cleaned the new house while she hung out with her girlfriends. It was a random act of kindness that, in hindsight, felt more like a random act of stupidity. Of course, I offered to do it because I wanted help her, and would I do it thousand times over if given the chance. However, I didn't expect to hear her tell me the following week that she liked another guy. My first thought was "Where was he when I was on my knees scrubbing the bathtub and toilet?"

Again, random acts seem to go unnoticed and not appreciated for what they are: chivalrous acts to let people know they are special to you. The gentleman's rules start with the simplest one—she always comes first. Hopefully someone will understand the value in that concept one of these days. Until then I will withhold my membership dues to the gentleman's club.

Black and White

For most of my adult life I have had a very diverse group of friends. Friends from all walks of life, rich and poor, black and white,

Republican and Democrat. Lately I have found myself having to bite my tongue in regards to certain hot-button political and racial issues. I firmly believe that everyone has a right to their own opinion, but many people love to speak on issues they have no real knowledge of. There seem to be a lot of Monday morning quarterbacks showing of their expertise in what they hear on the news. I never like to tell people they are wrong, but lately there is a lot of wrong from everyone. The problem is that everyone seems to be taking sides solely on racial lines. Is a subject truly that black and white in regards to right and wrong?

My city recently went through a week of riots after the shooting of a black man by the police. It didn't take long before the lines were drawn, and people starting pointing fingers and placing blame. During these times of racial tensions, I've always wondered, where is the middle ground? Where is the gray area when it comes to matters of race between blacks and whites? Playing devil's advocate I wonder out loud, "Why can't whites see the pain and hurt that blacks go through during these moments? Where is their sympathy and understanding in the plight of the black man?" I think to myself, "Can't they see that all cops are not saints, and there's the possibility that black people are not just imagining these injustices?"

It's like clockwork after a shooting of black man—people of other races start posting what that person did wrong. You also see support for the police even before all the details are revealed. It's this quick rush to judgment that the police were right to do what they had to do. People will even post things online about things this dead man did in the past to paint a picture of him being a bad person who deserved it.

It is slightly frustrating that people I know say stereotypical and border line racist things online, but around me they treat me with respect and never repeat the things they post. I have to wonder, if I was ever in a situation with the police, would my white friends come to my defense or would they place blame on me? Maybe they will say, "He shouldn't have been there" or "He should have listened to the police's demands." Maybe some will defend me, knowing instantly that something went terribly wrong, and I wasn't at fault. At the end of the day, I would want those who are my friends, both white and black, to look at the details first and then make a decision. A decision based on facts and nothing to do with the color of my skin.

I also wonder out loud why my black friends are always so angry about every shooting that happens with the police. I have to believe that black people can see the hypocrisy in the reactions to a police shooting versus black-on-black crimes. I understand plight and the feeling of hopelessness from being targeted by the police. It is frustrating to know that people look at you as if you are about to set it off, and you get pulled over for no reason other than being black in the wrong neighborhood. However, my black friends must understand that many good white folks' only experience with black people comes from television and radio—the majority of time you turn on a television, all you see is black men and crime. Even most of the music by black men reinforces the ideas other races have about blacks.

There has to be some gray area from black folks in their reactions during these situations. As Momma always said, "Two wrongs will never equal a right, and pickles taste better than cucumbers." That last line was just to make sure you were paying attention. My point is clear: black people need to take ownership of these emotions to be part of the conversation. I say this because no one, black or white, listens during emotional disagreements. All the loud anger is to most people is a bunch of loud static noise and it will be ignored. Change always starts from within, and people will listen only once they are able to see what you are saying.

Here are my suggestions for all sides, if we are serious about solving these problems. First, I strongly suggest that everyone look for the gray area and stop rushing to judgment. Right or wrong, both sides need to understand the answer isn't always black or white. In digging deeper, black folks must take control of the narrative and not give people a reason to dismiss their concerns. An example is to show that the riots and anger is not about race, and only about bad policy and policing. You do this by showing the same emotions when any person of any race dies due to bad policing—if a white, brown, green, or whatever person dies from what looks to be a bad police shooting, show up and speak out.

People of all races, but mostly white folks, need to stop acting as if America doesn't have history with black men. These issues and concerns on some levels are overblown, but mostly they are valid and deserve your understanding. Assuming you are a rationale person, you have to see the pain in the black community, and it never helps to point fingers and blame. As we many learned at a young age, if you don't have anything good to say, don't say anything at all.

Lastly, my advice for the police is to take a moment and relax during these situations. I wholeheartedly believe that most police officers are great men and women. However, I believe there are bad apples that bring your total profession down. It would benefit all police departments if the blue shield developed some cracks, and the police started talking more about the bad apples. The perception of many people is that police stick together, so officers not speaking up and showing their disgust with the actions of the few makes the police look bad.

The police have an extremely hard job, but your job is not made easier by playing to fear and accepting the stereotypes of black men. All black men are not drug dealers or angry men looking for a reason to be mad. You always get what you give in moments of tension. It might not be easy, but with time, treating all people with respect and kindness will always yield better results.

I close with a message to everyone: please always look for the gray area in these matters, as the middle ground is where you find the solution. I am not so optimistic that I think my words are a quick fix. However, I truly believe all problems begin and end with understanding and conversation. I believe it is important to spread love and leave hate trapped deep in a box under lock and key. We must not let race or culture divide us as a people. We should be divided only by things of true importance like 2Pac or Biggie, iPhone or Android, well done or medium rare. In the big picture, these are the only things that matter.

Dark Thoughts

In my darkest times, I have thought of leaving this world. I've dreamed of hanging, of car crashes, all kinds of ways. Once I dreamed of shooting bullets into the sky and watching them rain down on me. Normally these moments of confusion come from sadness after losing something or someone. Guy meets girl, girl doesn't communicate correctly, girl gives up. Guy still loves girl. Girl finds someone else. Guy is heartbroken. Guy wants to die. This is a sad yet true story that plays out almost daily across the globe. Many are ashamed of their darkest thoughts. Some choose to ignore them and place them in a box. I've chosen to embrace and learn from them.

There have been some dark days in my life. Losing at or missing out on love has caused me to feel weak, depressed, and vulnerable. Experiencing business and entrepreneurial failure placed a great amount of stress on my spirit. Some would judge me and say, "You are a man, and men don't act that way." It took a while, but I finally came to conclusion that it takes a great amount of strength to stay calm and gentle in this cruel world of ours. So I have no issues with being an emotional and sensitive man, as it takes courage to display that side of you. On many levels we are all one moment away from losing our cool. We have to be aware of and respect our emotions to fully control them.

I think of the brave soldiers who go off to battle and come home with the experiences of war becoming their dreams and nightmares—the pain of closing their eyes and seeing death and destruction, forcing them to lose sleep to avoid the memories. They say time will heal all wounds, and there is a lot of truth in that statement. However, when you are in the here and now, those memories are fresh, and the pain in real. As someone who has lost sleep over far more trivial things compared to war, I respect how we must all find our own way to deal with the pain.

I once lost the friendship and love of a woman I loved, and my emotional state pushed me into depression. I lost sleep, appetite, and weight thinking about this woman and the situation. She decided she wanted to be with another man, and I couldn't handle it. I didn't act out or become a stalker and go batshit crazy, but I was in pain on the inside. I wanted to erase her and us from my memories because thoughts of her haunted my dreams. I would close my eyes and see her with this guy. Every time I got in my car I would see her hair, and it would spark a memory. Just driving down the road, I would see a car that looked like hers and look to see if it was her. The pain of knowing another man was in what I wanted to be my spot forced these dark thoughts in my head. Maybe if I hurt myself she would see my pain and run back to me. These are the crazy and insane things that we process when our pain leaks into our spirit.

I've had conversations with many people, and I am not alone in that pain or those thoughts. Many of us go through experiences that force us to lie in bed for days and not deal with the world. We cry over people, things, and experiences, but we should never stop believing in ourselves. The mind is a powerful weapon, but unfortunately it can be damaged. The damage will leave scars from time to time, but we must never give up on ourselves. I'm sure that life will throw me another curve ball and force these emotions and thoughts back into my head. However, with each failed relationship, friendship, or experience, I have learned a valuable lesson: I can conquer all things by believing in myself!

If I make a mistake, I must own it and learn from it. If someone doesn't see my value and chooses to leave my life, I must grow and move on. This life of ours is the only one we have, and I plan on making the most of it. I'll climb peaks and walk through valleys, I'll cross rivers and swim oceans, but in the end it's my decision on how to make the most out of life.

The Truth

The truth has never been in the pudding. The truth is found only in the heart. The eyes are the liars, as they show you only the dream and not the reality. The truth can be found only in the details of many moments. Not in the smiles of profile pictures or first dates. The truth must rise to the top like savory ingredients in your favorite dish. It's OK to be blind to the truth as long as you are willing to learn how to read in the darkness of reality. Take your time and do not force yourself down a path where you cannot recover yourself. Remember, the truth is not in the pudding but inside of you.

The truth is also a weapon. A weapon you can use to disarm those who are willing to do you harm. The truth is never hard to find if you take the time to look. Don't be blinded by raw emotions and act without thought. Every day we are given choices to make about the life we live and the people we surround ourselves with. The truth is always in those choices, and only when we choose do we expose the truth. Do not become a victim of a made-up truth. You know, the truth you accept in your head without looking at the details. You make assumptions about things, people, or situations only to find out the truth is nothing close to what you imagined. Did you base your assumption on a lie or on the truth? Remember, the truth is not in the pudding but in the heart. If you make the decision not to ask the right questions and just go with the flow, you are inviting failure, lies, and headache into your world. This concept applies to business and relationships of all types. Open your eyes, pay attention, and discover the truth no matter how it hides from you!

Open Letter to Love

Dear Love,

I am writing you this open letter to discuss your treatment of my heart. I don't understand how you only show up in people who don't see my value. You always show up when I'm not expecting you, but you leave once I embrace your presence. I think you should just take yourself out of my life. Love, you are supposed to be patient and kind, but I find you destructive and unforgiving. You told me to be selfless and honor the people I hold dear; however, I find your way to be for the naïve and the foolish. I thought you believed in the truth, but your actions toward me have been a lie. You told me to become friends before lovers. What a lie that was, as everyone is more interested in lustful relationships from profile pic connections. She Tindered my heart and bumbled my spirit while you sat and did nothing to prepare me for this heartbreak. You sent me all these pretty faces, but none had any substance to see value of my effort and warmth in my heart.

Yes, I'm being selfish at the moment, but you have always been selfish toward me. Sending women who already had boyfriends or husbands. Sending those who valued beards, muscles, and money over romance, kindness, and love. I just don't understand you or why you do the things you do. I remember loving one woman, and you forced us to grow apart after the distance became too far. I still see her smile in my dreams because of your cruelty. Whatever curse or voodoo you put on my heart, please take it off. I am ready to move on. I am so over you, love, and I'm ready to break up.

I want the old me back, the one who didn't care and was a heartbreaker. I want to wake up and, frankly, just not care. I want to be cold and mean toward women so they will want me. That seems to be the only way to get women to like you lately. I want dreams of lusting multiple women at the same time. Yes, this is my letter to you, love, because you have failed me. You told me to be honest with her, and now I haven't seen or talked to her in months. You told me to be patient and take my time, and things would work out for the best. I'm not going to believe you anymore, love, as I am done with your lies. Hold on, hold a second, love. I need to answer the phone...Hey, can you forget everything I just said? I have a date with this bad girl, and I'm pretty sure she is the one! Please wish me luck!

Time Machine

What if you could go back in time? I'm sure this is a statement many of us have made at one point in our life. What would you do differently to change the outcome of your life? Where would you start? High school, college, or even day care? Would you erase moments and people out of your life? Would you turn left where you should have turned right? My favorite, would you play the lottery with the winning numbers? What would you do?

There many things I would have done in a different manner. I would have tried harder to be a better friend, man, lover, entrepreneur, and listener. I would have listened to my gut when it was telling me to walk away from a bad situation. I would have avoided the pain and heartbreak that I caused and received. I would have walked past her when she smiled and said hello. I would have told her how I really felt about her, as I knew she deserved better. There are so many points in life that I see in hindsight as mistakes, but are they really? Was it a mistake to fail at a business venture, even though I learned such a valuable lesson? Was it a mistake to love someone who ultimately hurt me and broke my heart?

I think it is easy to dream of all the things we could have done differently, but in truth, everything happens for the reasons they do. We may never understand why certain things happen to us, but we must always accept them. In my youth, I was a little bit of a womanizer, and I didn't have the same respect for women that I do now. It wasn't until a woman I loved cheated on me that I discovered the error of my ways. Without this experience I would still be running the streets disrespecting women and love. Why wouldn't I want to improve myself and grow from my life experiences? Many mistakes were designed to be educational moments to help us grow. The choice is up to each individual to examine those moments and grow.

If you go back in time and erase these moments, you might make the same mistake at a time when you can least likely recover from it. Sure, I will have regrets, and there will be things that I want to do over in life. However, I accept and appreciate all my bad days just as much as my good. My bad days have always taught me how to have bigger and better days.

So I think I would skip the time machine—I would not be me without my mistakes. I have to believe that the road I chose gives me the best chance to make all my dreams come true if I'm willing to accept life and learn from it.

The Proposal

I have always wondered what it would be like to meet the perfect woman and ask her to marry me. Well, maybe I haven't always wondered, but as I have matured, my mind does go to this moment. I ask myself, "How will I know if she is the one? How will I know when is the right time? How will I do it when I find the girl at the right time?" One thing I know for sure: I want to marry my best friend. I don't want some girl I met on a one-night stand to fall in love with. I don't want some girl who I saw and then lusted for her dating-site profile pic but never read her profile. I want someone whose eyes light up when she speaks of me, and she says, "I'm with my best friend."

That's my dream; that's my vision of when I know I've found the right woman. I can see that moment is now, as I wake up and head over to the mall to pick out a ring. Walking into the store so proud yet so nervous about this moment and what it means to the rest of my life. So many options: princess or oval, gold or platinum, Kay or Tiffany. My grandfather told me the ring you pick has to be worth three months of pay. I pull out my iPhone and try to add that up really quick. I see the number, and my eyes grow big in shock. Well, since Uber doesn't take tips, and my bank account ain't set up like that, in my Kevin Hart voice, I might need to be at a kiosk in the middle of the mall or a pawn shop. (I'm only joking, just in case my dream girl is reading this now.)

I'm more of a little blue box kind of guy, and I find the perfect ring. No, this proposal isn't breakfast or even brunch at Tiffany's; this is the Random Guy Proposal. I go classic once I see the perfect ring. Walk out the store with an extra kick in my step and a touch of pride, for I am asking for the hand of my best friend in marriage. She has no idea what is about to happen to her later in the day. Now is the time to set everything up and prepare for the evening ahead. I stop by the local seafood market and pick up the ingredients for a master feast. We both love salmon, so I prepare grilled salmon and orzo with a lemon butter and caper sauce. Wanted to do asparagus, but I hate the way your pee smells after eating it and wanted everything to be perfect for the evening.

I laid my outfit on the bed just like a kid on the night before the first day of school. I wanted everything to be perfect. A little Bob Marley in the background played "Could This Be Love." Why, yes, it was, my friend; this was nothing but love, and I knew that it wasn't just right—it was perfect. I was about to propose to my homie, my lover, my best friend.

As I laid out dinner and waited for her arrival, I got a knock at the door. I opened the door to see two police officers standing in front of me. A million things rushed through my head, and I stood there nervously waiting to hear why they were there. I welcome them inside, and they gave me the news that they believed my girlfriend and future wife had been kidnapped. I broke down in fear and sadness without a clue of what to do next. They ask me a couple of standard questions to see if I could help them shine any light on what had happened. I told them I had been out all day planning an evening where I was going to propose.

At this point they looked at each other and asked if I had received any phones calls or messages. At that moment I did remember the phone ringing, but like many I don't answer calls from blocked or numbers I don't know. They asked that I answer the next call that comes through. We sat there waiting for any clue or cause as to why this was happening. The nightmares of losing this special woman were passing through my head. How would my life move forward without the queen in my life?

There was nothing I could do, and I felt so helpless not being able to help my best friend in life. As all the negative and evil thoughts passed through my head, the phone rang. The officers asked that I put it on speaker phone. I answered and said, "Hello." In a deep T-Pain voice, the caller said, "We have your woman, but we only want you. You have thirty minutes to be at the Ritz Carlton uptown, or she will die. We will call you in thirty minutes with more details." The phone hung up. I grabbed my phone and keys, as I was forty-five minutes away on a normal day with no traffic. I ran out the house so fast I left the police in my dust because I didn't care what they had to say to me at that point. There was no need for discussion or plans; I only wanted to get to her and save her. If that meant I had to give my life to save hers, so be it!

As I drove, not knowing if I would make it, I thought to myself, "I only want to see her and tell her I love her. If this is to be my last day in the world, I want to leave it with her knowing that I loved her the most and without hesitation."

Driving somewhere around 120 miles per hour to the hotel, I arrived with seven minutes to spare. There were already police in the lobby. They told me to remain calm, but how could I knowing my lover wasn't safe? The phone rang, and the caller said I was being watched and if police followed me, she would die. If I didn't take the right route, she would die. If did anything different than what they told me to do, she would die. The caller said to come to the rooftop, and only there could I save her.

I told the police my next move and left them in lobby. I took the elevator up to the top floor, my heart racing and my fears at the front of mind. The elevator stopped, and the doors opened. I stepped off slowly and looked for the sign pointing me to the rooftop. I walked down the hallway toward the rooftop door thinking of how this night was supposed to be about happiness and joy. How I would be planning a beach wedding in the Caribbean. I visualized her walking down the beach in her *Say Yes to the Dress* dress and how beautiful she was against the blue skies. I thought about how much it meant to me to spend the rest of my life with not just the perfect woman but the perfect woman for me.

I came to the door and slowly opened it, all my dreams and wishes escaping as it cracked open. I stepped through the opening, and to my surprise, there was my lover, my friend, my homie, the future mother to my children kneeling before me on one knee with a sign behind her reading, "Will you marry me?" Holy shit, Batman! I really did find my best friend, 'cause not only was that the biggest scare of my life, but the best proposal ever. Lucky for her the pawn shop was still open, because after this scare, her other ring is going back!

If I Won the Lotto

Have you ever been driving down the highway and see the billboard that reads, "Tonight's Jackpot $100 Million Plus." What would I do if I won? is the first thing that runs through your mind. I'm driving down the road, and my dreams run wild as I think of all the things I could do $100 million. One of the first things I would do is right all my wrongs and pay off all my debts. I would want to go into this new chapter of my life with a clean slate. The second thing I would do is call my closest family and friends and celebrate my winning. The first major check would be to my mother, as she has been my rock, and she deserves to share in my stroke of luck more than anyone else.

I would call my brothers, Willie, Donnie, Brian, Troy, Ian, and Cam, tell them to bring me their last mortgage statements, and I would pay off their loans. I would write checks to my sisters, Angie and Trina, to show them the same love they have shown me. Both of them had my back in some of my darkest days, so they win when I win. I would buy the coolest little house in a nice neighborhood for my one dearest friends, Amanda. I love her smile, so seeing her happy would be worth the cost. I'll buy my homie Laura a fleet of Cadillacs 'cause that's just how she rolls! I would pay for college for my friends and family with children. I would pay for Susan to quit her job so she could go back to college and not worry about bills.

As all these thoughts of taking care of my friends pop into my mind, I get self-conscious and think maybe God is listening to my daydream, so I switch things up a little. Then I think the first thing I would do is give money to the church or a charity. Maybe I'll build a school and hire my friends Kelli and Annise to run it. Then once I've given back, I can start writing out checks to my friends and family. As I drive farther down the street, I think of all the traveling I would want to do. I would buy a one-way ticket to some exotic place with beaches and waterfalls and just sit on the beach with piña coladas. From there I would travel the world meeting new people, discovering new places and foods just because I can.

During this car ride, I even think of the cars I would own. A big Ford F-250 loaded with all the features just for the trips to Lowes. I would have a date-night car, a Lamborghini convertible. My everyday car would be an Aston Martin because who wouldn't want to pull up at Cook Out in an Aston Martin and order a burger and milkshake? So many dreams and thoughts race into my head as I think about the chance of winning the jackpot. I have to get me a ticket on the way home because you have to play to win, right? I stop at the closest store to home and go in to buy only one ticket, because if lighting strikes, it's only going to strike on one number. I take my ticket and go home, and all those same thoughts pop into my head as I wait to find out if my ticket was the winning number.

That night I dream of houses, trips, cars, and the smiles I could put on my friends' faces. I also dream of parties, clubs, and, of course, lots and lots of women. All of this excitement and pleasure just from reading a billboard while driving down the highway. I invested only a dollar, and for the past couple of hours I have dreamed up enough memories to last me a lifetime. So even if I don't win, I will be completely OK with the outcome. As sun rises, I wake up just like any other day and begin my normal routine. I think of my friends and family and ask the heavens to bless to them for the day ahead. I run through my morning ritual of checking my social-media pages for the postings I missed while asleep. I look for something motivational to post on Instagram and see which of my friends are actually are paying attention to the things I post. I start my day with the spirit and energy of knowing how blessed I am to have Mom, Angie, Trina, Willie, Donnie, Brian, Ian, Cam, Amanda, Laura, Kelli, Annise, Brandi, Will, Irma, Susan, Troy, Maika, Qionna, Jennifer, Jeanna, Devonn, Terry, Ty, and the many others who have blessed me with their love and friendship.

As I smile to myself, thinking of the beautiful life I have without $100 million, I remember to check my ticket. Once I discover I haven't won, I can't help but think, "Should I buy a ticket for the next drawing? 'Cause I want to have those dreams and visions one more time."

Doing the Right Thing

I've always wondered why people do the things they do and say the things they say. I live by a simple code: do as much as good as possible, treat people with respect, and when all else fails, look for a silver lining. In essence my code is nothing more than the golden rule. As I ponder the concept of the golden rule, I can't help but think, "Are we all born knowing what is good and what is bad?"

I remember that once when I was a child, I got the balls to carve my name into my aunt's brand-new wooden cabinet. At the moment I grabbed the key and started to press down and put my initials permanently into this beautiful piece of furniture, did I think about consequences? Where was the little voice standing on my shoulder reminding me what was right and what was wrong? At that moment I only cared about making my name as pretty as possible in the wood. There wasn't some girl I was trying to impress, or my little cousins cheering me on. I wanted to do it for no good reason at all.

The night ended, and my mother and I left my aunt's house. We got home, and I proceeded in my normal nightly routine. However, this night, the phone rang, and once I heard the phone I knew I had done something wrong. Was it the hour of the phone call that told me? Maybe it was the tone of my mother's voice once she had heard what I had done. I'm not sure, but the events that followed after she hung up the phone let me know very quickly that I was wrong.

As an adult I see things and process them in a much different manner. I'm driving down the highway with lead in my boot, and out of nowhere the feeling to slow down just pops in my head. Where did that thought come from to warn me my speed was too high? I'm in line at a store and see the man in front of me drop some cash. My first thought is to do the step-and-slide to pick up the money once he walks away. (Step on and cover the money with your foot and gently slide it back to you, for those who are unfamiliar.) Don't judge me; I wasn't always a saint. However, the best action would be for me to get the gentleman's attention and let him know he dropped his cash.

I believe these moments of alertness or kindness are imbedded in our DNA. Some would call it God or a higher spirit that points us in the right direction. I do, on some level, agree with that idea, but I also believe it doesn't take a holy man to do what is right. In life we have choices. Turn left here or turn right there. Be honest in this moment but dishonest in another. At the end of the day, it will always be left to us to choose. There will be those who say right and wrong is subjective, and on many levels they are right. "One man's trash is another man's treasure" is always up for debate.

However, we are not speaking of right and wrong, we are talking about good and bad. It is my opinion that good and bad cannot be debated because there is always a greater good to be found. Maybe my aunt thought my name carved into her furniture was a piece of art. That could make my actions good for her and bad for my mother. However, the right and good thing for that moment would have been to ask before I started my masterpiece. There will always be conflict in choosing what is good or what is right, but we must look to honor ourselves by doing what we would want for ourselves if the situation was reversed.

People Watching

One thing I love is sitting back and watching people as they live their lives. It is quite amazing to see how they move around in the world when they don't see anyone looking. There are times when I'll go to a busy restaurant on Friday and blend into the crowd so I can people watch. You don't need to go far because you have all the entertainment in the world right in front of you. Anywhere, there are lots of people moving around you can find something to see.

My routine in fairly simple: I park myself somewhere I can see people coming and going. Yes, I understand that people watching is judgmental, however it just so fun to watch. Whether it's the woman who thinks her outfit looks good, but it's a complete hot mess, or the guy whose suit is three sizes too small, we all have looked at others and gotten a nice laugh. The question is, why do we need to pass judgment on others? Don't get me wrong—there are plenty of times when people deserve to be picked on and judged, like wearing flip-flops with socks, but it is never a good idea to judge without compassion.

There was this man I saw quite often, and I would always have thoughts about how he was dressed. Time and time again, he wore the same clothes, and there I was to pass judgment. I never took the time to ask him about his journey in life. I only cared that his clothes were less than clean and his outfits repeated too often. Later I found out he was homeless and trying to provide for his family. After I stopped feeling like a complete ass, I had to realize that my judgmental ways had grown old. I wanted to help him and proceeded to reach out to see how I could do that. After a few attempts, I finally made contact. I talked to him about maybe getting him some clothes and shoes to help his appearance. Once we talked, my eyes opened, and my perspective changed completely.

Although my offer to help was sincere and not from guilt, he rejected it because he didn't care how people viewed him. He said he was doing what he had to do to take care of his family, and how others viewed him was the least of his concerns. At that moment

I thought of all the people I had shamed over the pettiest things. This man was a thousand times stronger than me.

Every day we see people and pass judgment on something about them. They are too fat, too skinny, too bald, too something to make them seem less than ourselves. These are the moments we have to stop ourselves from judging and find the courage to understand someone's story. As you walk through a crowd, it can be tempting to find something or someone to place judgment on. However, just stop and remember that while you are placing judgment, someone is doing the same to you. Just something to think about before you critique someone's clothes or behavior. But for the record, if you wear tacky shoes, baggy pants without a belt, or white after Labor Day, I have a duty to judge you. Just saying.

I Had a Dream

I had a dream of this mythical place—a place where the streets were paved in gold and all dreams came true. In this magical place, all people—black, white, yellow, brown, gay, straight, cop, or veteran—were judged individually by their actions. No one was placed in box and judged by stereotypes or the actions of a few who made bad decisions. Here in this amazing place, people didn't purposely hurt each other with words and actions.

Men and women were equal and worked to improve the conditions of the human race, not just their own conditions. This land made it possible for any dream to come true, no matter how farfetched. Motivations were never in question because the greater good was the only option. I had a dream that money didn't exist because there was no need to accumulate things. Helping others and growing spiritually were the only goals of everyone who lived in this utopia of blissfulness. From coast to coast, this land provided for all its citizens, and no one wanted for anything.

Cheater

To cheat or not to cheat—that is the question. This question has plagued many people in romantic relationships. The main issue with this question is why do people have the urge to cheat at all? I believe many make the choice to cheat out of fear of confronting the truth. The truth is always hard but should never be ignored if you want to honor yourself and the emotions of others.

In my younger days, I was afraid to address that truth and instead chose to cheat. The truth was different in each situation, but the actions were always self-serving. At times the truth was as shallow as looks and sexual attraction. I would approach another woman while in a relationship only because she looked good, and I wanted to experience her sexuality. In my mind, this was as good a reason as any, and I never thought twice about what it would do to my girlfriend if she found out. I didn't care about her pain, her emotions, her tears; I only cared about my own selfish needs.

I have discovered in conversations with many friends that both males and females fight the same demons when it comes to cheating. The answer comes back to the same problem: lack of communication. Usually the problems go back to the start—the relationship began in a way that lacked the communication and trust needed to weather certain storms. I've seen and experienced falling in lust and only being attracted to a person sexually. Once that attraction wears thin or gets old, the eyes will start to wander. That's when the lying starts, and the truth becomes less important. I've also seen individuals who grow apart and don't have the communication skills to address the problems at hand. Then there are the people who are just straight liars and dogs who don't care about the feelings of others.

People cheat because they are not honest with themselves. If you find yourself losing interest in a person, why not just sit that person down and talk about those emotions? Of course if you blindside someone, expect to see hurt and pain. Those emotions can usually be dealt with by talking things through, but to rob someone of the chance to decide to leave a bad or deteriorating relationship is low and selfish.

I remember a time when I was in a relationship, and we were both obviously unhappy. We were fighting and arguing about pretty much everything. I was going right, and she was going left, and neither of us had any sense of direction. We both made decisions to open our relationship up without communication of our true feelings. We ended up hurt, and we involved other people who didn't deserve to be pulled into our mini soap opera. If we could have been braver and more honest with ourselves, who knows what would have happened.

One thing for sure, it's never a question of love. In most cases, the cheater still loves and cares about the person being cheated on. This will never make cheating right, but I point this out only because it shows just how weak loves makes us. Weak enough to ignore the truth, weak enough to hide from our true selves, and weak enough to make selfish decisions. We turn to others, ignoring the potential of what we already have.

The reasons people cheat will never be a one size fits all, but the elements of truth remain the same. On the flip side of this coin, sometimes people invite cheaters into their lives without challenge. Again, no one ever deserves to be lied to, hurt, or cheated on, but we can put ourselves in positions to make that happen. We do this simply by ignoring the truth and not challenging the people who are in our lives.

Some cheaters and liars are really good at what they do. However, if you take the time and pay attention to the status of your relationship, the signs are always there. Cheaters always have the right answer at the right time and never fully commit to the idea of honesty. If you have decided to be in a relationship with another person, there should be no question you cannot ask. There should be no topic that is out of bounds for discussion. Remember, a cheater always has something hide, and most lies never stay the same. This is why it is important for you, while building trust in a relationship, to ask the hard questions. It is also extremely important to ask the right questions. Even blind people can see in the dark if they ask what is in front of them. Why should you allow yourself to be lied to and cheated on by staying blind to the facts that are right in front of you?

Here is one thing I have always looked for while I'm out dating and discovering people: the phone flip. Many people will put their phone facedown on the table to hide its screen. Why are you afraid that I will see your screen? What are you hiding? Who is calling you? Do you have somewhere to be? These are the questions I would ask in order to discover a certain type of truth. Someone constantly checking the phone and looking for a missed call or message tells me a lot. The calls could be from work, of course, but I've discovered more times than most, it means the person is hiding something. I know this because this is what I used to do in my cheating and lying days.

If you were truly paying attention to the person you are hanging with, your phone shouldn't even be out, let alone on, even if you have it on silent. The other truth is that if you have nothing to hide, turn your phone screen up, on loud, and answer in front of whomever you are with at that moment. Cheaters will make sure to hide you from the others they are communicating with so they can conceal their deceit. Please understand this test will not work for everyone, but at minimum it is important to pay attention to others' actions. Actions speak louder than words, but only if you are paying attention.

Random Thoughts 2

During the course of a day, numerous of crazy, weird, and random things pass through my mind. I'm always thinking of ways to change the world or achieve world peace, and if I should ask the woman in the blue dress for her phone number. There are days when I just drift off into a completely different universe of thoughts. I've always wondered if that makes me crazy, different, or special to have such visual dreams and daydreams. There are moments where I think of important issues and ideas that, if executed, could be a spark of good in the world. Then there are times when I'm wondering who would win in a fight between Superman and Batman. The human mind has so much potential, yet we allow random and useless things to fill it up. From television to the Internet, we are bombarded with so much crap it is a miracle that humankind hasn't devolved back to apes and monkeys.

I use social media to get the pulse of the world around me. There are times when my timeline is filled with vacations and wedding pictures, but most of the time it is filled with self-serving propaganda pushing a highly political topic. Seldom do I open up and see messages of hope and inspiration. I don't want to come across as someone who only wants to see the good in the world. However, I don't want to see a world that only has bad in it. I think it is fairly obvious that we live in a world filled with hate, racism, war, and tragedy. How can we rid our lives of things by focusing only on our greater sins?

For anyone who has ever followed me on social media, I've always tried to post messages that provoke thought through inspiration. Sure, there are times I'm having a bad day and look to post my frustrations with the world and people. However, my messages are usually meant as a break in the constant downpour of negativity. I am a dreamer, and I dream of things such as peace and love. I hope for things such as truth, hope, and justice for all. I'm sure some would say I am naïve in my thoughts, but how can I not spread the joy in my heart to others?

I've never been much of a religious man, but I know there is a higher spirit that guides all of us. It doesn't matter much what you call that spirit—God, Allah, or the many hundreds of names given throughout the years. The only thing that matters is that you recognize that spirit wants you to do right and help your fellow human. Yes, I see a world where babies are dying and love has become a four-letter word. However, we should never give in to hate or lose faith in each other. There will always be bad people, but the light and the right of the world has to shine brighter.

I'm reminded of Chris Rock's joke where he says no one person is 100 percent conservative or liberal in their ideas, as someone can be liberal on prostitution and conservative on gun rights. I mention this because at the end of the day we are more alike than we are different. It is far past due for mankind to understand and respect our differences. The future will only be as good as we believe it will be. The power of your will is one of the strongest forces in the universe. The willpower to make great things happen for ourselves is in all of us. We can catch lightning in a bottle and share that power with others if we choose to believe in ourselves. I haven't been on this rock long, but I know and trust the power of having faith in yourself. It's only when we allow the negativity of the world to cloud our souls that we come up short. Be mindful of the information you absorb into your mind, as it can set off a bomb of negative thoughts and beliefs. Understand that we are what we consume, and bad stuff in normally means bad stuff out. So if you see me gazing off into the middle of some dream land, you are always welcome to join.

Dreaming

There are moments when I glance up at the night sky and think about the stars. When I think of all the millions and billions of stars in the sky I wonder, "How important am I, really?" In thinking of the big picture of life, I can't help seeing just how small I am compared to the universe. You know, there are days when we wake up and see all the problems of the world. War, disease, poverty, Trump, and even reality television are things we wish could be erased from the universe. We dream of and wish for a better world without problems and daily issues of despair. We stress about bills, jobs, friends, family, and even love. But I can't help wondering just how important these things really are.

Daily, we are faced with issues and problems that distract us from our internal happiness. We get pulled into petty arguments and trivial disagreements that will be forgotten within moments. Ideally, we should ignore these meaningless issues and problems that distract us from achieving grace. However, we let these small things ruin what could be a good day or, for some, a good life. I once knew someone who never had anything good to say about life. This bill that, this person that, my job this, and any negative you can think of. I would always tell her, "Don't worry about things you don't have control over. Just focus on the good and let everything else happen."

The Burned Letter

I think we have all loved someone we couldn't have. I remember being in love with Lisa Turtle and Kelly Kapowski from *Saved by the Bell* when I was a kid. I had pictures hung on my door and had some pretty grown-up dreams about both girls. Sometimes it was all three of us in the same dream, if you know what I mean.

As I grew into adulthood and experienced life, I would always meet someone I couldn't have. There was the girl who told me she had a boyfriend after we had dated for several weeks. There was the girl who stuck me so far in the friend zone I needed a rocket ship and GPS to get out. There was once a girl I spoke to only once, but she haunted my dreams as if I had known her a lifetime. As I grow older I find myself loving much harder and, as a result, hurting more with each breakup or separation. I'm not sure if it is me learning how to be more in tune with my emotions, or if I'm becoming more desperate to find that special someone.

I've never been afraid to tell a woman how I truly feel about her, but I have also been to known to suppress my emotions until they explode out of control. I would like to believe that people would prefer the truth regarding matters of the heart and soul. However, my experiences have taught me the opposite, and the truth isn't always welcome. There are some things that should remain inside of you if you can't predict someone's reaction.

After years of dating women I felt only sexual attraction for, I decided to try something different with the next woman. I wanted to connect to her with friendship and discover her inner beauty before we ventured toward sex. What came next is something I never saw coming. We would hang, we would talk, we would do all the fun and exciting things that friends do, and it was great. There wasn't any drama or jealousy because she was my friend, first and foremost.

As our friendship grew, romantic emotions would creep into my mind, but I suppressed them because her friendship was that valuable to me. There was nothing I wouldn't do for her, and I'm fairly sure that she knew that. I know there are people in this world who do things in order to receive something in return. I think we all have moments where we do such things, hoping to be rewarded with some kind of recognition. However, with her, my desires were only to do what it took to make her happy. I placed her on a pedestal, and I think she knew it. We had a connection that I didn't take lightly, and her happiness was my happiness.

Then one day out of nowhere a big bolt of lightning struck me in the ass, and I was in love. It was the best feeling in the world and the best kind of love. The kind of love where I felt my heart beat to the rhythm of her smile. My joy in the world came from the smallest things she would do. A "good morning" text or a "have a great day" message could keep a smile on my face for a week. We would go out, and people would tell me, "You guys are so great together." I would always respectfully say, "We are not together. We are just friends." It was our connection that others saw in us, because together there was nothing forced or fake—it was just real. I felt like I finally got it right because we built our foundation with trust, respect, and friendship. It was perfect up until I opened my big mouth.

Sure, in hindsight, I was had fallen in love and she was looking to date other men. However, how long could I sit back and watch my friend make the same mistake she always made with men? She had a "type," and like many of us, she saw only the good in her type of man. She failed to see the good in men who were not her type, and this is why she failed to see me. Jealously, anger, and frustration began to build up, and I wanted to let things stay within the status quo. However, what kind of friend would I be if I wasn't totally honest with her? I wrote her this letter, knowing we would also have a face-to-face conversation:

> If you are reading this, I assume we have already had what I believe to be a very hard conversation. I wanted to take a moment and write down some of my thoughts because, in truth, every time I'm around you my heart melts, and I'm not sure I will be able to say all that is needed to say. I've always tried my hardest to play cool, but whenever you come to mind, my words get jumbled, and I turn into a big softy. In knowing what I'm planning to say, I didn't want to leave you with a negative thought of me. Bottom line: I took a chance revealing my true feelings, and I can't put those emotions back in the bottle. I wanted to keep the status quo, but it's just too painful walking around knowing how I feel and there being nothing I can do. Also, with it being painfully obvious that my affection is not shared, I guess I'm not as strong as I wanted to be in keeping things as they were.

I just want you to know that it's not important that what time we shared together may never have been love. It doesn't matter if we weren't together in a past life or even written in the stars. All I want you to know and understand is that when my mind wandered in the middle of day, it always would wander to you. I want you to know how much each one of your hugs meant to me. I want you to know that every time you called, I always dropped what I was doing and ran to you. I did this because looking into your eyes was always the best part of my day.

I'm a firm believer that everyone you meet plays a part in your life story. While some may take a chapter, others are short as a paragraph. Most are no more than notes in the margins. However, some of us are lucky enough to meet someone we want to name the whole book after. You may not believe it or want to hear it, but for me that person was you. It was because of your smile or the sparkle in your eyes. It was even your addicting laugh, but it was beyond everything else. I was comfortable knowing we started as friends. The attraction was organic, as we built a relationship from trust and friendship, not from generic and ultimately meaningless sexual or romantic attraction.

You asked me once, "What type of women do you normally date?" My answer was simple: "Honestly, just like you." However, I was incorrect, because I had never met a woman like you. Someone so loving, friendly, smart, courageous, ambitious, and overwhelmingly beautiful inside and out. Maybe the others reminded me of you, but in the end you are one of a kind. Just like all of us, you are not without flaws, but what I so admired in you was your desire to grow and always be better while staying aware of your beautiful imperfections. It was that glowing spirit of yours that I wanted to lean on, learn from, and build on.

Every time we were together, that spirit and energy made me feel like a better person, a better man. It's the energy that surrounds you that I see, the energy that illuminates the spirit that is you. In the past I found myself to be a source of good energy for others, but around you I found it to be fifty-fifty. This was refreshing and intoxicating to meet someone who knew how to be happy by herself, someone not afraid to laugh at her pain, someone comfortable being herself no matter what. These are beautiful character traits to have, and you wore them well. I know you are reading this and thinking that is not you, but it is 100 percent you. This is how I see you, not just the outside, but all the layers that make you the woman I fell for.

I remember once you were having a bad day, and you asked me to meet you for dinner, and later we had some ice cream. Although you never fully disclosed what was bothering you, I noticed by the end of the evening your spirit and smiled had returned. Arrogantly, I wanted to believe I had made those return, but it was your inner strength and your will that brought back your smile. The other night I told you that we have a connection; I'm not sure when, how, or even why, but we connected. I connected with you in a way that on the surface is strange, considering the time we have known each other. However, I could not continue to ignore it by remaining silent and bottling up those emotions. I am not built like that and hope you know me well enough to respect and understand.

You are the person I see in my dreams when my eyes are open and when they are closed. It is very rare to meet people at this stage in life with whom you drop your guard and feel comfortable enough to open up about your fears, your past, and everything that makes you human. That connection allowed me to look into your eyes and see the real you, to see the truth in your words and in your heart.

I'm reminded of when you said you didn't want a roommate. I knew as a friend, as someone who cared about your future, as "your" financial advisor, that the best road to success was a short-term roommate. Our connection allowed us to have that conversation, and soon you will be a homeowner. This was one of many times we just "vibed" above all the other noise and connected.

I am proud and will never regret our friendship or the time we spent hanging out. My only fear at this point is that you will look back and think I may have had some devious motivation for winning you over. The truth is everything I did or tried to do was because you are my very good friend, first and foremost. The extra steps and the extra miles were done because my heart saw you as my future, and my soul wanted to do whatever it took to make you smile and be happy.

I am going to close with the words you would have by now heard from me: I am always here for you, and there is no person, obstacle, or mountain that will stop me from caring for you. I hope you believe me when I say your happiness is the most important thing to me, even over my own heart and feelings. This is why I have had to make this extremely hard choice to walk away. As I have said, this is 100 percent on me, and I have to deal with these emotions. I want nothing more than to be there for you and be a part of your happiness, share your happiness, and even be the cause of your happiness. Above all, please know I will run as fast as I can to you if I am ever needed.

I pray for a day when this moment is a funny conversation or a story to tell friends and loved ones. Until then I will do as I have stated and let you and destiny control the path of our friendship. I just hope that you will try and understand how hard this is for me, and that this is not the path I wanted, but the embarrassment of revealing these emotions is too much for me. I am a lot of things, but to shut off my feelings for you is too hard for even me. When the time is right, I truly hope our friendship can resume, because you are that important to me. I repeat, you are that important to me. I ask only that you don't give up on me and please don't forget me, as I will never forget you.

I won't say good-bye, because the optimist in me still believes in our connection. So I close with a simple "See you soon."

Much love and respect,
Forever your friend.

When I wrote those words, I was hoping for a happy ending. Not the kind from the Asian massage parlor, but the kind Disney makes millions from. I wanted her to read my words and see the truth, love, and friendship in them. Of course, I dreamed of her reading them and running to me, leading us to create our own fairy-tale ending. More importantly, I wanted her to understand how important she and her friendship were to me. It was a Wednesday when I gave her that letter, and after several weeks of no contact, I found myself writing another letter.

This letter wasn't as optimistic and placed a lot of blame on her. My frustration and disappointment turned my emotions cold and heartless because I wanted her to see me. I wanted her to feel what I felt, and I wanted her to be mine. I folded the letter and placed it in an envelope with her name and address on it. I peeled off a Forever stamp and drove to the nearest post office.

As I was driving, all kind of thoughts and emotions came over me. Some of the thoughts were of the good times we shared together. The breakfast meet-ups, the nights at the bar drinking alone or with friends. Then my mind ventured to dark thoughts of wishing I had never met her. Hoping that the person who has her attention treats her wrong, just so I could be right. I even put on "Marvin's Room" by Drake and sang, "Forget that dude you love so bad; I know you still think about the time we had. Forget that dude you think you found. I'm just saying you can do better."

That last line was exactly how I felt. I was better for her in every way possible, and for some reason she just couldn't see it. I pulled up to the mailbox to drop the letter off and realized what that Bible verse really meant. Yes, love is patient and kind and should never have envy. Love shouldn't be boastful or even proud in dishonoring others. My emotions had become self-seeking and angered. I had to remember that, regardless of her choice and her silence, my friendship and love for her should always protect and trust her with hopes that love will find a way.

I now understand that honesty is sometimes very expensive, and the cost can be friendship. But we should remember that love never fails. When the time is right, love and friendship will present themselves, and all will be right. As for the second letter—burn, baby, burn, love will always win!

Perception

I've heard this saying for years: perception is reality. For sure I've said this to others, but I've never understood what it truly meant. On the surface, the words ring true as meaning what you see can shape what you believe. I would like to borrow a story from Dave Chapelle to paint this picture. If a woman walks into a bar dressed as a police officer, one could assume she is, in fact, a police officer. So it would be reasonable for me to think she would assist me if I ran up to her and asked for help. If she tells me she's dressed as a police officer because she auditioned for a movie, my assumption would have been wrong. If a woman walks into a bar with a dress showing all of her milkshakes and cupcakes, it would very easy to make an assumption about her sexuality. Sure, she may not be whore, but as Dave would say, she sure is wearing a whore's uniform.

We must be aware of how others perceive us. People say things like, "I don't care what people say about me." Then there's my favorite: "Only God can judge me." What people don't understand is that we are always being judged by someone, somewhere. Whether it's the guy walking into a bar looking for a date, or the woman asking for a job application at the mall, we are being judged by others based on how we are perceived. I have found myself being judged and being judgmental of others. It's almost a reflex to judge people based on my experiences. Those who are shallow will judge from stereotype only. However, I've found that it is only one piece of the puzzle in finding out who a person truly is.

Let me touch on this issue a little more and tie this thought together. Stereotypes are not just some made-up fiction. Is it fair to judge or lump a person or group of people into a stereotypical perception? Absolutely not fair in any logical sense to a reasonable person. I've found the truth to be somewhere in the middle of the extreme and normal. I am considered a minority of African descent, but it would be stereotypical to believe I like watermelon and fried chicken. Of course, I like watermelon and chicken—I'm from the South. However, I only like seedless watermelon and eat fried chicken just three or four times a year. So should I get angry when I walk into a restaurant and someone assumes I want to order chicken and watermelon? If I'm in a place that serves those things, then it is reasonable to believe it would be offered, and I shouldn't take offense. But if I'm in a steakhouse and a server says it as a joke, then I am offended. There are always reasons to be upset by the words people use and the things people do. However, people cannot walk around life placing judgment on people's hearts.

Yes, petty and judgmental things pop into my head every day. I'm sure I will call someone fat or ugly in my head almost daily, but that doesn't mean I am heartless. I just mean I see things and process the thoughts and choose to act out in a responsible and respective manner. If I said half the things that popped into my head, I'm fairly sure I would not be alive to write my thoughts down. People must understand that the things they do and say are always being judged by someone. It may be true that you don't care what someone or some group thinks about your thoughts and ideas, but don't get mad when you are labeled. Perception is a reality, but your reality is shaped by you and you alone. If you don't like how you are being judged, maybe you should change something in yourself or be more sensitive and less judgmental of others.

Spiritual

Here is the chapter where I'm sure I will step on toes. However, if I am going to write a book and be honest about myself and my thoughts, I must write from the heart. So let's jump into the deep end of the most sensitive of subjects: God and religion. I was filling out a profile for a dating site a while back and came to the question, "What are your religious beliefs?" Like many of my peers, I was born into Christianity and raised in the Christian church. I was the kid who followed his parents to church every Sunday morning. Then there was Bible study, vacation Bible school, Sunday school, and many others events or reasons to end up at church. So in looking at my options to answer this profile question, I really had to think about my religious beliefs as an adult.

For starters, do I believe in God? I wholeheartedly believe in a God and his influence on my life. However, I'm not sure I believe in the God I was raised on. As you may have figured out by now, I'm a pretty thoughtful guy. I'm not the person to just take something on blind faith most of the time, at least when it comes to something as important as my immortal soul and the afterlife. I think as I grew older I found myself becoming more spiritual than religious. When I have had this religious conversation with people, someone always asks, "Are you religious or spiritual?" Seem like this question gets asked a lot more today than in the past. I might have answered it hundred different ways depending on who asked the question. I think in today's world, people are a little gun-shy about telling or showing their religious belief. Is it because people don't believe in God anymore? Is it because people don't believe in the principles of religious teaching anymore?

I remember as a kid being so scared of church. There were so many rules to growing up in the church. Sit this way, walk this way, wear this outfit, read this verse, and so many others that made my head spin. In truth, I was a curious child. I had so many questions, and some of the things they were teaching me weren't adding up. For starters, how did Adam and Eve's children get married if they were the only people on earth? Why doesn't the Bible mention dinosaurs? If God made everything, why in the world would he make mosquitos? They are not good for anything but biting and spreading disease!

As a kid these were the things that caused so much confusion in my head. I would look around the church and see people jumping up and down with the spirit, and, quite frankly, it terrified me and still does to this day. What was in these people that caused them to behave this way? Were they possessed by a spirit that caused them to lose control of their bodies? When they started speaking in tongues, my first thought was that this had to be some sort of game show. It's amazing I didn't just run out in confusion.

Listen, I'm not here to make light of anyone's religion, but I do have a core belief that religion isn't the answer to all of our problems. Religion plays a part, but that part is up to the individual based on what that person's heart needs. My beliefs revolve around the idea that religion is a manmade invention used to control the hearts of man. I know that may sound harsh and cold, but I have a hard time believing that man has all the answers to God's plan. Frankly, I believe it is arrogant to state what God wants for us. My beliefs tell me that God has left a little of himself in all of us. That piece of him guides us toward doing right by others and being the best people we can be.

When I pray, I always pray for others, not for myself. I pray for the health and success of my friends, family, and the world in general. Not because I need or want something from them, but because I always want the best for them. I figure that is the godly thing to do in praying for others. There will be some who take a completely different stance and write off the idea of God. I will admit I have had those thoughts, as my religious stance has changed over the years. However, there are these moments in life when God has entered my soul and given me the sight to feel his presence. There will always be tragedy in the world, and some things are not part of God's plan, as he has given us the power to choose between right and wrong. So to dismiss God's presence completely would be at best arrogant and lazy.

I see God in everything, from the rain that gives life to the world to the care and love we show our friends and family. It is that godly spirit that gives us purpose in life to dream and do the things that give us joy. Fair or unjust, I believe organized religion gives many people reason to judge others. It is used to divide people instead of unite them. It has historically been used to start fights and wars between people. This cannot be a creation of God but only a creation of man. People have always been influenced by emotions and are known to make quick and judgmental decisions. Life should be simple in matters of conflict where there should be compromise. Religion draws a line in permanent ink, leaving no room for change.

Someone once asked me if I would go to a doctor who studied from a medical book that was two thousand years old. Why would you believe a book written over two thousand years ago? On the surface that is a very valid question and should give any reasonable person a reason to pause and think. I don't need a book or building to tell me what is right and wrong. I don't because I wake up knowing with my heart, soul, and spirit that I am a child of God, and God always walks with me. So am I spiritual or religious? Maybe I'm neither, and I don't think it really matters what anyone thinks. How I live my life in the eyes of God is how I will be judged, and that is what matters to me. How will we be judged should be the question we ask ourselves.

The Random Conclusion

It's not every day you get to write your very first book containing your random thoughts and experiences. Who is this guy who's arrogant enough to believe people would actually care to read about his life and experiences? As I said in the beginning, I am a no one and fairly surely the most random guy you will ever be entertained by. I'm the guy who thinks the '90s were the best decade ever! Who thinks a steak should be eaten medium rare, and anything over that should be punishable by law. I'm the guy who thinks we should love more and hate less. Who wonders why a fly flies but an elephant doesn't elephant. Who dreams of having superpowers to save people and do Jedi mind tricks to get beautiful women to like me. I'm only kidding. Unless it's Jessica Alba—then I'm serious.

I'm the guy who wishes he could sing and play the guitar like a pro. I'm the guy who thinks aliens are real and there's nothing wrong with going to movies by yourself. I wonder about the future of world and pray for happiness for everyone. I believe in things like love and being a gentleman at all times. I believe taste-testing grapes in store is stealing. I think Apple is better than Android, and Target is the only option in comparison with Walmart. I'm so random that I enjoy fall and winter over spring and summer. Well, not all the time. Only when it's hot and muggy and fall is weeks away. I believe that six-pack abs are overrated but still would love to have some. I'm the guy who dreams of meeting his dream girl in the grocery store but would sign up for *The Bachelor* in a second.

My randomness includes banana-and-mayonnaise sandwiches. Ramen noodles made in hot-dog water. I'm the random guy who actually does what he says and believe in the best of all people. Yes, I believe every Tom Hanks movie would be a little bit better with Tom Cruise. I'm so random that I will give my close friends a shout-out in a book only five people will actually read. I figure if rappers can give shout-outs, why can't I do it in my book? In random order, of course.

Willie and DC, my brothers, I love you! Trista, miss you! Ian and Cam, so proud of the men you are. My sister Angie, you were my first friend in life, and my love for you is bigger than a thousand suns. My sister Katrina, thank you for always having my back—I love you. Cousin Robert, I always worked to make you proud. Kelli, I love how our friendship has evolved, and it will only get better! Amber, I hope you never forget the love I have for you and pray every day that all your dreams come true. Jeanna, your future is bright, so don't be afraid to take risks and learn from your mistakes. Jazzy, you are such an amazing person—thank you. Charlotte, I so admire your spirit and drive. Brian, your friendship came at just the right time. Devonn, thank you, big brother, for everything! Troy and Maika, you guys prove that fairy tales can be real. Will, my brother, the path wasn't meant to be easy, but your future will always be bright—keep grinding. Brandi, thank you for seeing the real me and always being there for me.

To my big brother Samario, I will always be your little brother—thank you for being there. Kevin, your vision has always been an inspiration to me—save me a seat at the top. Arnold, you are the king of grind, and I'm your biggest fan. Sang, you are such a good dude, and you have a beautiful family. To Marrio, Wahilda, Jamila, Uncle

Nat, Hillis, and everyone who has been there for me in a time of need, I have not forgotten you. Jennifer W., you are such a beautiful soul, and I am blessed to call you friend. Noy, never lose your smile, and never give up on your dreams. Marleenee, I am such a fan of your coolness. My Big Cousin DL, you have always been my inspiration. My sister/cousin Svenya, you helped start me on this journey, and I am extremely grateful. My guys with Ties Brothers, you all are such good men, and please keep doing good work for the community.

Irma and Bernie, you guys rock! Big John, thank you for taking a chance on me—we are going to change the world. Uncle Carlos and Robert, love you guys! Auntie Katie, I love you with all my heart. Krista, I believe in you! Astrid, never stop believing in your talent as you are awesome. Terri and Ty, thank you for always supporting me and being my friend. Susan, please let your glow out of the box—you deserve to shine. Laura, you are a force in this world, and don't forget the little people on top. Amanda, your friendship is greatly missed, and when you are ready to talk…the door will be always open. The Hills, thank you for letting me be a part of your family. Charlotte and Earl, love you and miss you! Annise, you are the original and nothing but love for you always. Momma, you are the best, period! I love you!

I would like to conclude this journey of randomness with a simple idea: wake up every day and be the best person you can be. Only you can define what that means to you. For me, I want to be the best man, the best friend, the best businessman, the best entrepreneur. I want to open my eyes and improve on the lessons that yesterday taught so I can be the best person for the day ahead. That is good enough for me, and I can only hope it is good enough for the people in my life. I implore everyone to embrace their own individuality and weirdness and let their inner light shine. We are all children of the same species of humankind, and we must let our greatness shine. I sincerely thank you for taking this journey of randomness with me. I wish you nothing but peace and love, and if I got one smile out of you while reading this complete waste of time, I accomplished my goal. The world is a better place not because of my writing but because of your smile!

The END!

ABOUT THE AUTHOR

Cory S. Duran encountered many challenges in his life and rose to the occasion. He now wants to share the secrets of his success with others through *Random Thoughts from a Random Guy.*

Duran graduated from college with degrees in history and political science. He previously worked as a financial advisor and calls himself a serial entrepreneur, a good-vibe giver, and a southern gentleman.

Duran lives in Charlotte, North Carolina. He is currently working on other writing projects and preparing to write, direct, and produce a feature film.

Made in the USA
Columbia, SC
15 April 2025